8-16-89

DO NOT REMOVE
CARDS FROM POCKET

The Whales
in
Lake Tanganyika

The Whales
in
Lake Tanganyika

LENNART HAGERFORS

Translated from the Swedish
by Anselm Hollo

GROVE PRESS
NEW YORK

Copyright © 1985 by Lennart Hagerfors

Translation copyright © 1989 by Anselm Hollo

Originally published in Swedish by P. A. Norstedt & Söners,
Stockholm, under the title VALARNA I TANGANYIKASJÖN

Published by Grove Press
a division of Wheatland Corporation
841 Broadway
New York, N.Y. 10003

Library of Congress Cataloging-in-Publication Data

Hagerfors, Lennart, 1946–
[Valarna i Tanganyikasjön. English]
The whales in Lake Tanganyika/Lennart Hagerfors ; translated
from the Swedish by Anselm Hollo. —1st ed.
Translation of: Valarna i Tanganyikasjön.
p.   cm.
ISBN 0-8021-1095-9
1. Stanley, Henry M. (Henry Morton) 1841–1904—Fiction.
I. Title.
PT9876.18.A3368V3513   1989   88-21641
839.7'374—dc19   CIP

Designed by Irving Perkins Associates

Manufactured in the United States of America

This book is printed on acid-free paper.

First Edition 1989

10   9   8   7   6   5   4   3   2   1

The Whales
in
Lake Tanganyika

Zanzibar

15 January 1871

This morning something happened that may change my life. On the other hand, it may just be my imagination, a monstrosity produced by my hung-over brain.

I was roused by a hard metallic voice in the alley outside the small house I've been renting for the last couple of months. Like a knife the voice cut through the calls and laughter of passersby; it even drowned out the yelling and wailing of my neighbors and their children.

"Mr. Shaw! Are you there?"

I raised myself up on one elbow. My throbbing head became aware of the unpleasant possibility of a forthcoming torrent of insolence from some underling at the British Consulate. They were given to harassing their less distinguished compatriots here on the island. But when the call came again, I heard a neutral, cold, distinctive quality in the voice that was more challenging than condescending.

With my other elbow I nudged the Negress I had bought on my first day in Zanzibar and indicated that she should go to the kitchen. She wrapped a dirty, limp piece of material round her hips and shuffled out, barefoot, leaving behind a sour odor of sweat, sex, and rancid oil.

As soon as I sat up, I broke out in a sweat. It seemed to be late in the morning, and outside the only window of the small gray room the sun's reflected light glimmered so powerfully I had to close my eyes. Behind my eyelids I saw a row of suns roll past, flashing their needle-sharp light into the tenderest spot of my brain. When I opened my eyes again, I was barely able to distinguish the familiar objects in my room: a wooden table, two chairs, my trunk, my accordion, the calabashes of palm wine, the whisky bottles, her foul-smelling bundles containing God knows what . . .

"Mr. Shaw! Are you in?"

For a moment, I had forgotten the voice. The reminder made me feel worse.

Then the door flew open, and a terrible blinding white light entered the room. Before I was able to raise my hand in front of my eyes, I glimpsed a figure bathed in this torrent of light. I got up and staggered into the dark beside the door.

"Mr. Shaw?"

"I'm here," I croaked, my voice still clogged by night phlegm.

A man stood before me. He was about thirty, short, with an uncommonly sullen heavyset face. There were sharp creases around his mouth; his cheekbones were high, his forehead high and wide. His body, small but compact, looked as if it had been cast in a single piece. He was not a handsome man.

It took a while for his eyes to adjust to the dark room. Then he turned to me, and for a moment I met his blue-gray gaze before it slowly moved on to examine my body. Something attracted his attention in the region of my crotch, and I looked down to see what it was. Through the fly of my underwear—the only garment I had on—my member was ridiculously pointing at the bed, as if longing to go back there. Under his eyes, which did not flinch for a second, I had to stuff the half-erect thing back in. It occurred to me it had been quite a while since I'd felt embarrassment.

"Excuse me."

"By all means."

He was standing very straight, left fist propped against his hip. The right hand held a short whip. He did not remove his topee. His clothes were plain but of good quality: boots of supple leather, strong khaki trousers, a fine cotton jacket.

After he had looked me over, he turned to examine the furnishings of my room, listened to the clatter in the kitchen, and cast a dry glance at my slave girl when curiosity impelled her to peek through the curtain that separated the two rooms. As I waved her away, my paralysis faded, and I pulled a chair up for him.

"What can I do for you?"

At first he seemed not to have heard my question but just stood there as if petrified by his own thoughts. Then he drew himself up, looked me in the eye, and started talking. He did not look away for a second, and he didn't blink once. His wide, craggy face remained immobile except for the droopy mustache, which bobbed up and down in an almost obscene manner.

"My name is Stanley. Henry Morton Stanley. I am a correspondent for an American paper, the *New York Herald*. Its manager, young James Gordon Bennett, Jr., has sent me out to lead an expedition into the heart of Africa. I am offering you the position of third man— you would be the third white man in the expedition. According to our plan, we will leave Zanzibar in a few weeks. You will be paid three hundred dollars a year, with the use of servants and a donkey specially purchased for your transportation. In return, I will expect you to assume responsibility for the boat I intend to take with me to Lake Tanganyika, to supervise porters and soldiers, and to perform, conscientiously, any task I assign to you. All in all, I expect you to dedicate your life to this expedition."

It was as if someone had arrived from the moon to inquire after my services. The *New York Herald*? An expedition into the heart of Africa? Nausea forced me to sit down on the chair I had offered him. My life as a sailor and my sojourn here on Zanzibar were both eventful and eventless enough for me to just quite manage them. Take a boat to Lake Tanganyika? Where was that?

Stanley strutted around me while attempting to describe my tasks, the organization of the expedition, supplies, et cetera. I wasn't listening. His voice sounded distant; all the rest of the world seemed to have congregated around that little spot in my brain whence my hangover came streaming. How had such a tremendous project been so vastly compressed and forced through the needle's eye of this hangover that was my consciousness, filled with boredom and emptiness?

And on top of it all, this curious man, who seemed overcharged with energy and talked as if the future had been implanted in the small of his back.

Wearily I asked, "How did you find me?"

"The British Consulate. They said you were a miserable wretch, lazy but not untalented. They said you'd be done for soon, unless something decisive happened in your life. Now it has happened. I have decided to take you along."

"Why?"

"I can use you. Come with me."

Just then, my Negress came slinking in from the kitchen with two mugs full of palm wine. Without a word, she set them on the table. She curtseyed quickly and then retreated backward, still bent over, so that her round breasts swung back and forth. Stanley took a long step forward, grabbed her arm, and pulled her to the middle of the room.

"She yours?"

I nodded, and he started palpating her like a naturalist examining some rare mammal for the first time. His arms stiffly outstretched, he squeezed her head, pinched her breasts and thighs. She stood stock-still, as if sniffing the air, ready to flee at the least sign of serious danger.

When he seemed satisfied, he uttered a short, shrill laugh and gave her a little shove in the direction of the kitchen. She was gone in a flash. He wiped his hands with his handkerchief and resumed his strolling around me and the table. Then he came to a halt in front of the mugs.

"You drink?"

7

"Sometimes."

Strangely enough, he looked amused.

"From now on, you'll have to keep your cravings under control."

Not once in my life have I longed for strenuous adventure, much less nurtured a dream of exploring the interior of Africa. Basically, I like my creature comforts and simple pleasures without being a true voluptuary. Hard labor I have always tried to avoid. There have been times when I've enjoyed performing small tasks on board a sturdy vessel, on days when the ocean is calm and the sky a peaceful dome. In port, it's mostly habit that leads me to have a good time drinking and whoring like all the others. I'm truly happy only on the few occasions I find time and peace enough to play my accordion.

Now something slammed shut. It felt as if I were trapped in a narrow pass, with an enormous tidal wave advancing on me. I sat there like a small cork trying to contain some unfathomable force. Someone had chosen me, perhaps by accident, to take part in and be in charge of something whose true extent I was far from comprehending. At the same time, I felt strangely detached from the offer, as though it hadn't really been made to me personally. I just happened to be there.

"What is the purpose of this expedition?"

"An explorer never knows in advance what he will discover. If he did, he really wouldn't have to travel, would he?"

Below the beard on my chin, I saw drops of sweat running over the substantial rolls of fat on my stomach and spreading into the folds between them. Now and again, a drop would catch in the hairs on my chest, swing there for a moment, and then roll down, dampening the waistband of my gray underpants. My hand lay on the table, curiously lifeless, and my bare feet on the packed earth floor looked like they belonged to someone else.

Stanley's boots came to a halt right in front of me. He called out a name, and a Negro servant rushed into the room and handed him a sheet of paper and a pen. Stanley laid these on the table in front of me and pointed to the bottom of the page. Without reading what it said, I wrote my name in the big damp stain his finger had left there.

"All right, then. From now on, you are under my command."

"What are we going to do in the interior of Africa?" I asked again.

He did not reply but turned and strode firmly through the light-drenched door. He had hardly left the room when the girl started weeping and wailing in the kitchen.

Only then did I realize what a thirst I had. I knocked back the two mugs of palm wine, one right after the other.

Zanzibar
1 February 1871

According to the calendar, it's been two weeks since Stanley hired me. They have been so eventful that I've lost my sense of time. Perhaps it was two *years* ago that we met in my shack? That moment and this do seem separated by the experiences of two years. Time's own motion, however, has swept onward like a storm: the two weeks have swirled away in a temporal space equivalent to two days.

My thoughts about this time are curiously detached. I haven't felt *present* for a single moment. My body has been ablaze with a fever of health. I have found myself at a distance, by the side of—by the side of whom?

Two years, two weeks, two days? What difference does it make? I'm with Stanley, and the two of us have fitted out our expedition.

Nothing has held us back. There is hardly a bazaar, marketplace, newly arrived vessel, dealer, or store we have not visited. Stanley is indefatigable. On our search for equipment we tramped through even the most squalid Negro quarters. The stench of excreta, rotting garbage, and fish in all possible stages of decomposition, smoke from open fires, and the odor of stale simmering foods assailed us in the narrow alleys. Dirty children covered with sores, their bellies swollen, their navels huge, came running out of the derelict shacks and begged insistently. Stanley shooed them off with his whip, I used my knees and arms. Our calves grew numb as we plodded through the loose sand, and sweat streamed from our pores (or rather, mine—Stanley's skin seems too dry for perspiration). Never in my life have I imbibed so much water—*water!*

It hasn't been much easier in the Arab quarters, not to mention the part of town inhabited by Muslim Indians. There, in winding alleys between whitewashed buildings, gateways, and alcoves, with slaves standing guard at the entrances and silent harem women tiptoeing around inner courtyards piled high with bales of cotton fabric and ivory stacked like firewood, next to tools, metal wire, and glass beads in boxes and baskets heaped on top of one another—*there* I sweated for other reasons. The Oriental's inscrutable, patient, and superior stare, his ability to generate insecurity and impatience in Europeans, the feeling that he knows something no one else knows—all this made me uncomfortable. They move with cool dignity, well aware of the deep wells of sensual pleasure available to them in the form of power and honor, food and women, and, above all, wealth. They're treacherous, all of them, but enviable.

Dealing with them, even Stanley became nervous and awkward. During discussions about price and quality, his jaw muscles twitched and the knuckles on his whip hand turned white. He looked as if he were about to explode. Sometimes his pallor and a dry fit of coughing showed that the explosion had taken place inside him. Damned Arabs!

Occasionally Farquhar came with us. William L. Farquhar is Stanley's second-in-command, thus my immediate superior. His appointment causes me to believe that even Stanley can make mistakes. Farquhar has been drunk every single day—he's even worse than I was. He is tall and fat, quite a bit fatter than myself, and sports a short straggly goatee on his ruddy face. Constant alcohol fumes waft from his mouth.

I did, once, point out his unsuitability to Stanley, but he just laughed.

"Don't worry. On the caravan trail, many miles from Zanzibar's insalubrious bars, his qualities as a good sailor and sharp mathematician will prove invaluable to us."

Sailor and mathematician? On an expedition to the interior of Africa? Stanley's way of planning is so detailed and inscrutable that even I, who get to observe his thinking at close quarters, find it hard to understand.

At first I thought that Farquhar had some kind of hold on Stanley, not knowing how else to explain his calm and assured behavior. Now I'm ashamed of that suspicion. It would rather seem the other way around. The first time I met Farquhar, he gave me an amused, shiny-eyed look and said:

"So, there's two of us sailors in this caravan."

Then he laughed mirthlessly. Stanley found his

remark amusing. But I still wonder what inner qualities the man possesses, what Stanley really sees in him. For the time being, I treat him with respect.

So far, I have learned the names of only three of the Negroes Stanley has hired. One of them is Bombay, a strong, tough-looking fellow with graying hair. He has been chosen as the captain of the guard, the soldiers. Under him there are a number of subalterns, of whom I know only Mabruki by name. I noticed him because of his infirmity: one of his hands is crippled. It seems he was once left hanging from a tree limb by his wrists as a punishment.

The third isn't really a Negro but an Arab. As his interpreter and personal valet, Stanley has employed a handsome Arab boy named Selim.

Both Bombay and Mabruki seem to have taken part in an earlier expedition, one led by two men named Burton and Speke, if I heard Stanley right.

No half-breeds have been hired. Stanley has taught me to see what despicable creatures they are: unreliable, sycophantic, and cruel, lacking any goals in life. They have no character and cannot be used as porters, soldiers, or officers. The only thing that stirs them into action is their lasciviousness. On this island, no other group procreates so assiduously.

There were a few days when I hardly saw Stanley. He was paying calls on both the American and the British consuls. The latter is a Dr. Kirk, of whom Stanley speaks with respectful dislike. One day, when I met him after a visit to Dr. Kirk, Stanley looked irritable but brightened upon seeing me.

"You're a good, simple, straightforward fellow," he

said, and punched my arm. Despite some slight pain—
he happened to hit a nerve—his appreciation pleased
me.

Well, everything is ready for our departure. All our
provisions are in a gigantic warehouse owned by Webb,
the American consul. Their volume is so enormous that
it is hard to fathom how they'll be transported to the
interior of the continent. Just the mountains of cloth
bales, which will be used as currency to pay for food-
stuffs and as tribute to local chiefs, represent a mone-
tary value ten times greater than what I'll be able to
earn in a lifetime. In addition to those, we'll carry
victuals, cooking utensils, two disassembled boats,
ropes, string, tents, saddles, sailcloth, tar, tools, ammunition, firearms, mattocks, medical supplies, bed-
clothes, presents for the chieftains, and some special
supplies for us white men, such as spare clothes, articles
for personal hygiene, and delicacies.

In addition, Stanley purchased twenty-two donkeys,
all of them without saddles. At last there was something
for Farquhar to do: in a surprisingly short time, he
manufactured a saddle for each and every one.

The last few days I have hardly spoken with Stanley.
This is only due to circumstance, since Farquhar's work
on the saddles, and his calculations of the amounts of
food we'll need, have obliged Stanley to spend more
time with him than with me. One afternoon, when he
hadn't said a word to me all day and we were about to
part in front of his house, he looked at me for a long
while with those gray-blue eyes that never seemed to
blink. Then he said:

"Well, Shaw, we'll soon find out what manner of man

you are. In Ujiji, in the midst of the deepest darkness, you may catch a glimpse of the light. Then we shall see if you can prove yourself worthy of that gift."

I must have looked hopelessly confused, because he uttered an embarrassed little laugh and slapped me on the cheek, quite hard but in a comradely fashion. Then he did an about-face and strode into his house. Whatever he was alluding to, I did not feel worthy of it.

Otherwise, I've noticed that people I don't know have started greeting me in the streets and alleys. They know who I am: one of the leaders of the greatest expedition that has ever left Zanzibar for Bagamoyo, our starting point on the mainland. I'm often invited to have a drink.

Now it is night. In just a few days, we'll embark on boats for Bagamoyo, where we'll stay until we have hired our porters. I feel lonely tonight. I have already sold my slave girl to my next-door neighbor, an insufferable half-breed, proprietor of the worst saloon in all Zanzibar. He had been ogling her for a long time, and he offered me an inflated price. She stood there and cried, the way Negroes do; she's really quite young still, but I'm sure she'll be happy with her new master. At this moment, however, I miss her. With the money I got for her, I intend to throw a bit of a bash for some of my friends before I leave.

A couple of hours ago I took a bottle and wandered along one of Zanzibar's prettiest beaches, all by myself. I felt abandoned, I wanted to cry. It's strange. Now that everything is supposed to begin and I'm about to grow up to be a real man with a goal in life, it feels as if I had come to an end.

I threw up on the sand. I don't want to go. That's it.

The sea breeze was wonderfully fresh, but there I was, vomiting. The waves were slapping softly against the shore, and farther out I could see the silhouettes of boats on the sound between Zanzibar and the mainland. Everything seemed so simple and self-evident. But I did not belong there. I was a mistake. How on earth could Stanley take on the likes of Farquhar and me?

"There's a thirty-three-point-thirty-three percent chance of survival on an expedition to the interior of Africa," Farquhar announced the other day, with a revolting grin. He's the mathematician.

When I returned home, my stomach felt empty and demanding. As I don't have any food in the house, or anyone to prepare it for me, I was forced to go over to the damned half-breed. He greeted me with a contented smile and told me he'd already tried her several times.

"Got a bargain," he said.

I saw her for a moment before she disappeared behind a curtain. She gave me a hate-filled glance. I could have killed both of them.

My thoughts make me sweat, and I have to run out and empty my bladder time and again. Goddamned whore! Goddamned half-breed! Tomorrow it will be a joy to talk to Stanley. And to get going at last.

This will be all for now—but writing consoles me. Outside my shabby house, the African night stands dense and dark, full of stale, salty air. Full of secrets, too. The glowworms know. The crickets' calls echo between the buildings. Other sounds I can't identify enter through my only window. Out there—over there—past forests, savannahs, and mountains, the greater darkness is waiting. It is inhabited, in a tight, magical, physically close community, by Negroes who have never seen the ocean. I don't belong there.

The Negroes here in Zanzibar sometimes laugh at me, as if they knew something about me. I don't know anything about them.

I think about my homeland, about the first bite into a Christmas apple, about cold damp morning fog on a paved street, about the warmth inside a pub as big snowflakes descend outside. I even think about my mother in her Sunday best and the long walks we took, me holding her hand, while Father lay at home sleeping off his Saturday-night drunk.

Bagamoyo

15 February 1871

It has been almost a fortnight since I've written anything. I haven't had the strength. All of it has gone into
dealing with one day at a time, one hour at a time. I
haven't even touched my accordion. It isn't time I lack;
peace of mind is what I don't have. I search for solitude
but suffer from it, I avoid the company of others while
yearning for companionship.

Here in Bagamoyo, Farquhar and I have been quar-
tered in our own small rooms in the back of the house
Stanley has taken over. In front, in the open yard that
marks the beginning and end of the caravan route, the
tents have been pitched. Behind the house, Stanley has
ordered the construction of an enclosure to contain the
expedition's animals. And all of this is patrolled by
soldiers who keep thieves and curiosity seekers at bay.

From early in the morning until late in the evening—
even at night, in fact—the house is enveloped in insufferable noise. Donkeys bray, soldiers shout and laugh,
goats bleat, pigs grunt—all the time! The stench of

animal dung is hard to bear too, as my only window opens onto the corral.

Nights I sleep fitfully, and in the daytime I have to endure the sarcastic glances of the soldiers. But no one says anything about it anymore.

My last night in Zanzibar began with a group of whites, mostly British sailors, who had been passing the time together in bars and bazaars. The intention was to celebrate Farquhar's departure as well as mine. Everybody kept buying rounds, but it was like indulging yourself at a dinner after a funeral. I felt completely empty. What was missing? The everyday? The adventures to come did not fill me with anticipation. Instead, I was already missing my secure daily routine. It felt a bit like having one of your ears stopped up, only on a larger scale.

"Look at that Shaw, he sure looks grim," someone remarked.

"Now, don't look so pale, me lad," said someone else. "Have another, and enjoy your fame to come!"

We kept eating and drinking all night and didn't part until three in the morning. I walked home—home?—and tried to get some sleep. In vain: I was suffering from an intolerable itch over my whole body.

After tossing and turning for more than half an hour, I got up, lit a small stable lantern, and prepared to go outside. There was a gentle knock on the door. I opened it and raised the lantern to see who it was: Farquhar.

"I won't be going," he declared.

We stood there and stared at each other. My lantern lit his face from below: it was grotesquely puffy, dark shadows contrasting with yellowish bulges of bare skin.

I started laughing so hard that I had to stagger back to the bed as Farquhar sat down quietly on one of the chairs. I couldn't stop laughing. Farquhar's words had pulled the stopper, and with my laughter the whole expedition—every last glass bead, every flintlock musket—streamed out of my body.

"I'm not going either. Stanley can do it alone. He's a different breed."

Not much else was said. We got up and stumbled out into the tropical night like sleepwalkers. It was pitch dark. The stable lantern cast a yellowish glow on the walls of houses, where grotesque shadows of our legs took gigantic strides. In silence, we walked through empty alleys. A dog slunk past us carrying something in his mouth, a few goats huddled against a wall, and chickens gave warning clucks in the courtyards. Passing one house, we heard an infant crying; in another, a woman was sobbing desperately. Only one dog barked at us. I felt at home.

We ended up at a little bar close to the beach. We woke its Indian owner and asked him for a bottle. He handed it to us without a word, took the money, and went back to bed.

And there we sat, Farquhar and I, on the ramshackle verandah, waiting for dawn. The air was cool and raw. We didn't say much. Coughed, drank, smoked our pipes.

At dawn, the color of the sea grew lighter. A grayish mist lay over the beach, where a couple of Negroes walked past with fishing nets. A few seagulls were up bright and early, screaming and diving into the surf. From a nearby hut a young woman emerged. She yawned, stretched, pulled up her wrap, and hunkered down. A naked little boy toddled through the doorway behind her, stopped on the threshold, and let fly with a long stream out of his tiny member. When they were both done, she softly bent down to the child, put him on her hip, and went back into the hut. I saw her teeth flash as she smiled at him. They looked like they were living a good life.

It was a morning with a very special light. Never before had I found the beaches of Zanzibar so beautiful.

In half an hour, the sun broke through the mist, and people started appearing in the alley. Listening to their chatter, I could make out the occasional mention of Stanley's name. Our host came out and gave us a glum look. We ordered another bottle and something to eat. Reluctantly, he brought us some of yesterday's rice patties and a bottle of maize spirits that tasted appalling.

Two hours later, when my drunkenness and my hangover had joined forces, we saw people heading down to the harbor. They seemed lively, in a festive mood. We turned our backs to them, and no one paid any attention to us.

When silence had returned to the alleys and huts around us, our host reappeared, looking as if he had just swallowed a live toad. He informed us curtly that he was closing up because he too wanted to go down to the harbor to watch the departure of the expedition. Farquhar raised his hand and waved the man away. He hurried off in apparent fright, with his wife in tow.

After we had been sitting there for a while, Farquhar got to his feet, picked up the empty bottle, and walked out into the alley. He threw the bottle against a wall, hard, making it explode in a shower of splintered glass.

Then he came back, panting and even redder in the face than usual, and flung himself into his chair.

We did not speak. It was midmorning, and silence reigned, an unreal silence. Even the animals seemed quiet. They crawled into corners, leaned against walls, lay still with their eyes open. It was like an eclipse in full daylight.

The only sounds were a persistent little whistling in one of Farquhar's nostrils and the remote hubbub from the harbor. It seemed to me that we sat there for hours on end.

Finally I heard voices drawing closer. Bombay appeared in the alley, accompanied by four sturdy soldiers. A bunch of half-grown boys swarmed around them, eager to see what would happen. Bombay was carrying a whip, and the soldiers had rifles. Their eyes shone with malicious glee. Only Bombay's gaze was cold and impassive.

"Mistah Stanley he say you come boat," he drawled in a monotone.

"Tell him he can go by himself. We're staying here," I replied, my words lacking the conviction I wanted them to carry.

I felt a stinging pain. In my stupefied state, I did not at first realize what had happened. The bleeding stripe on my arm made me comprehend that Bombay had used the whip. A Negro had struck me with a whip!

A short fracas ensued. Farquhar pulled his pistol, I threw myself at Bombay. We were rendered harmless in a couple of seconds. Farquhar took a vigorous swipe across the mouth, and my shirt was torn to shreds by the soldiers. We surrendered immediately. Farquhar

underwent a strange transformation. He drew himself
up, his puffy face taut and determined despite the
blood trickling from a corner of his mouth. The soldiers let go of him, looking embarrassed. Then, calm
and dignified, he strode down the alley toward the
harbor. With the butts of their rifles, the soldiers
guided me in the same direction.

Where did Farquhar find his dignity, his strength?
Bombay led the way, followed by Farquhar. Some
thirty yards behind, I staggered along, bare-chested,
surrounded by soldiers and boys of all ages making
faces and chattering like monkeys. The first quarter of
a mile we didn't see one other human being, but ahead
of us, in the better parts of town, the hubbub grew
louder. I tried to lengthen my stride to catch up with
Farquhar but did not even get close. Just as he turned a
corner, the noise grew incredibly loud. People were
shouting, laughing, singing. The next moment it was
my turn. I looked back to plead with the soldiers but
could hardly form the words before a rifle butt in the
neck and a kick in the arse made me stumble in front of
all those people. The jubilation grew louder.

There were people everywhere: on the rooftops, by
the road, at the windows, up in the palm trees. The
colorful splendor of their clothing was set off by the
white walls of the cube-shaped buildings. It was all joy
and festivity, enhanced by the additional spice of this
unexpected entertainment. People were shouting like
madmen. I glimpsed faces of all colors, from black to
white, and all of them, it seemed to me, were distorted
by malicious glee and hostility. Some were frighteningly
angry. Why?

Farther down, by the shore, a short distance from the
boats that lay anchored in the shallows, stood a large
group of prominent Europeans, men in white suits and
women in light-colored gowns. Between them and the
boats stood one man, arms crossed on his chest: Stanley. The short whip stuck out from under one arm.

I saw everything as if through a film of streaming
water. The noise was so loud that there were moments
when I couldn't hear it anymore. I don't know whether
I was laughing or crying, but I must have been doing
something, because one of the soldiers slapped me on
the mouth and shouted at me to be quiet. I remember
that because I was surprised I had been making any
sound at all.

Then I concentrated on getting over to Stanley,
afraid that the mob would tear me to pieces. They tried
to slap and strike me, some were even throwing stones.
As I staggered across the sand toward Stanley, I saw
him as my liberator. No one else could save me. When at
last I stood in front of him, he rapped me across the
chest with his whip and pointed at one of the boats.

"Get into the boat, man!" he shouted in a falsetto
voice.

I gathered my courage. I had nothing to lose. Every
eye was upon us, but I didn't give a damn. I barely
noticed that the uproar had been followed by a strange
silence.

"Would it not be best if I stayed? Look at me. I'm
worthless."

Stanley laughed and turned to the other white people as if sharing a joke. But I saw that most of them just
looked embarrassed. Then he became serious and
roared:

24

"Into the boat, man! We have a contract!"

He struck me again, much harder this time. Then Farquhar intervened. I don't know what would have happened had he not done so. His voice dark and calm—where did he find it?—he said to me:

"Come on, Shaw. Let's get into that boat. We've signed our lives away."

He took my arm and led me to the boat. Slowly we waded through the surf. He helped me over the gunwale, and I crumpled onto the deck.

There I lay for a long time, curled up, safe from all eyes. Farquhar sat next to me but said nothing. My wounds were stinging, and I was plagued by thirst. All around there were voices shouting and giving commands, donkeys braying, horses whinnying. Stanley's shrill falsetto could be heard now and again. Men and animals splashed through the water, the surf sounded steady, and once in a while it rocked the boat. Farquhar gave me water before I found the strength to ask for some.

When the sun was at its zenith, the hubbub rose again. I felt the boat abruptly detach itself from the beach and bob out through the surf. Gradually the cheers and singing died away, replaced by the slap of waves against the hull. The wind carried the panic-stricken complaints of donkeys on other boats across the water. I heard the fear of creatures who found themselves out of their true element.

Then I fell asleep in the shade of a coat that Farquhar had rigged up for us.

Bagamoyo

16 March 1871

Resignation feels good. The first days here in Bagamoyo were terrible. I did not leave my room except for trips to the latrine. Even then, and every time, I was the butt of the soldiers' jokes. As soon as they saw me, they started reeling about, weeping, laughing hysterically, and an easily amused audience gathered around us.

On the second day after our arrival I got a fever. The welts made by the whip became infected and festered. The one across my chest, from Stanley's whip, was particularly troublesome. Farquhar, serious and glum, came to my room each day and tended my wounds, and each day, as he left, he said to me:

"Come on, resign yourself. Assume your duties!"

It sounded like a magic formula. Once I threw a bloody, pus-stained bandage at him. He enjoys my weakness.

On the fourth day after our arrival on the mainland Stanley appeared on the threshold of my room. For a long time his blue-gray eyes looked at me without blinking. How does he manage that? Don't his eyeballs dry out? On this day he was particularly bright-eyed because he had just visited the French Jesuits on the outskirts of Bagamoyo. They keep a cellar of French wines. He sat down on a crate next to my bed and told me about vintages and dishes I had never heard of before. He was enchanted by it all, like a child.

Suddenly he jumped to his feet. I thought he was leaving, but he stopped by my small window, his back turned to me. He crossed his arms, and his entire body tensed like a spring.

"We have to be strong, Shaw! Strong and determined. We white men bear a great responsibility."

He gave a long and solemn speech about the tempering of the will and the evils of weakness. There was nothing particularly surprising in what he said; it was the kind of talk all men in authority tend to deliver. Yet the manner was remarkable. He spoke with a shrill rage, as if he were standing in a gigantic auditorium trying to convince a hostile audience that they were wrong. He seemed to have forgotten me entirely.

Then he fell silent and let the words reverberate in my tiny room. After a while he sat down on the edge of my cot and tried to take my hand. Instinctively I shrank back against the wall and pulled my hand away. Now his voice was a hiss.

"I am strong. I am a demanding, stern, but just father to our entire caravan—to the Negroes in particular. I know how important it is to have a father, because I never had one. Nor scarcely a mother. I know."

I had to suppress a giggle, and his eyes widened. I found it wildly comical that Stanley had ever been a child. He breathed on me, long steady breaths. The wine and garlic fumes made me feel dizzy and nauseous. I hadn't had much to eat for several days.

"But I *am* weak," I said. "So why take me? Take someone who is strong instead!"

He got up, put his fists on his hips, and stared at the ceiling. It was as if we were acting in a play.

"Trust me. I know what I'm doing. Even weakness has its place, provided it isn't apathy. The strong destroy one another or battle themselves into a deadlock. But in motion, in the tension between strength and weakness, that is where deeds can be accomplished. Without opposites, there is no dynamic. And that is why you, Shaw, must strive for strength."

"And you for weakness?"

He smiled indulgently.

"No. I am subject to other laws. I am strong and strive for strength. I am the bright light that looks for the feeble light. I am the clear thought that looks for the clear feeling. I am the hardness that looks for a softness as strong as my own hardness . . ."

So many dark words. I gave up trying to follow them. Perhaps it was my feverish state that made his speech seem bathetic and overblown. At the same time, it frightened me. I knew already that there was a hidden menace in everything Stanley said. I understood, lying there on my cot, that his every word was only a prelude to action. I felt threatened, and the stale air around us heightened that feeling. Stanley was preparing me for something. What was it? For him, talk without action was like eating without swallowing your food.

"Today you will get back on your feet again. Listen, Shaw, we shall restore your authority as well as your health—you and I together."

He said this with a mild smile, in the same guileless tone one might use to wish someone many happy returns.

"But I'm ill."

"Get up!"

His voice was hard now; there wasn't a trace of that intimate tone left. At first I didn't understand what he meant, and simply stared at him in fright. When he grabbed his whip, I sat up out of sheer reflex.

"On your feet!"

I felt dizzy.

"You stink! Your body stinks, your soul stinks. I shall cleanse you!"

And cleanse me he did. It was horrifying. In order to break my listless fever trance and return to reality, I had to cross over into an even more unreal state; I was forced from a dream through a nightmare and then out into the real world again.

He led me to the front of the house, then seated himself on a chair in the shade next to the building. He ordered Bombay to round up all the soldiers and other personnel to form a half-circle in the open yard. I was told to stand in the middle of that great arc. It was midafternoon, hot and dusty, and I had trouble adjusting to the glare.

Stanley asked if the soldiers had been laughing at me and mocking me. When I nodded yes, he ordered

Bombay to hand me the long donkey whip. I took it with limp fingers. (These goddamned whips!)

"Now call out the one who has been laughing the most and give him a good hiding! Make it snappy!"

Everything had happened so quickly. Four days I had been lying there alone, hardly even eating. Now, all of a sudden, I was exposed before everyone and had been told, for the first time in my life, to use a whip on another human being.

"But sir, don't you think this can be resolved in a more dignified manner?" I asked, trying to sound accommodating.

"No, it cannot. You'll either give a whipping or get one. Your choice."

As I turned to the soldiers, my eyes met the sarcastic gaze of that huge fellow Asmani. He had been the worst offender. His laughter had been pure scorn, without a trace of the others' humor and frivolity. Next to him stood little Saburi, a sycophantic type whom I suspected of inciting Asmani and the rest, of being the real culprit behind it all. Now, of course, he was looking at me as if butter wouldn't melt in his mouth.

I ordered him to step forward. He did not seem surprised by my choice and went down on all fours without being told to do so. I swung the whip with all the strength I was able to muster in my weakened state. The lash slid lazily across his back, and the tip twitched a little in the sand beside him, like a sun-dazed snake slithering away. Asmani and a couple of others laughed out loud. I tried again and again, but I couldn't get the hang of the whip.

"Bombay! Show him how it's done!"

Looking bored, Bombay took the whip and hit the ground in front of me with a violent snap. I shrank back, and they laughed some more.

"Bombay! On his back!"

Bombay turned his furrowed stone face to Stanley and asked:

"What him punish for?"

"None of your business! On his back!"

The lash brought out a stripe of blood on Saburi's dusky back. His body shivered, but he did not utter a sound. The whip was handed back to me, and I raised it. Still on all fours, Saburi turned his head and gave me a serious look. His gaze didn't flinch even though I lashed out at his face. Once in a while I scored a hit, but mostly I missed. I also began to have my doubts whether Saburi really was the most guilty one. Maybe he was just the opposite. When I finally got the hang of the whip, I was exhausted. And my authority was far from restored.

At that moment a rage surged up inside me of which I had not believed myself capable. It was a question of them or me. I returned the whip to Bombay, grabbed his rifle, and ordered Asmani to step forward. I put the muzzle against his temple and told him, with Selim interpreting:

"I am a kind man. I am not used to handling whips. But anyone who mocks me or disobeys me will get a bullet through his skull. And you, Asmani, will be the first."

He saw my rage or, God knows, madness and went gray in the face.

"Beg for mercy, on your knees, and I'll spare your life. But I won't do that the next time!"

He begged for his life.

I handed the rifle back and staggered to my room, where I threw up bile. I had hardly lain down on the cot when Stanley reappeared in the doorway.

"That was the interior cleansing. Now for the exterior!"

My legs were jelly, but I had to follow him again, this time to his private washroom, where Selim was pouring water into the bathtub. In spite of my delirium, I was relieved. So the exterior cleansing was simply a bath, nothing worse. I would take a bath in Stanley's very own tub!

After Selim left the room, I took off my clothes. Stanley told me where to put them, pointing with his whip. When I was in the water, Selim returned with a box of soap and clean garments. He took away the soiled ones.

My wounds were stinging, and I was trying to avoid getting soap in them, but Stanley didn't miss a trick: with his whip, he pointed out the spots I had to scrub and took care to see that the wounds were properly cleaned. That done, he ordered me out of the tub and watched me get dressed in silence.

"Tonight you and Farquhar will dine with me. I'll send for you when it is time."

Soon after dusk Selim came to tell us dinner was served. There was no table talk. Stanley heaped my plate. Afterward, he poured two glasses of gin for Farquhar and me. He didn't have any himself.

"Well, Shaw, tomorrow it's back to work. Goodnight, gentlemen."

Outside, in the darkness, I vomited up the food and alcohol. My stomach hadn't been ready for either.

Stanley is a curious man. It took him only a few hours to get me back on my feet. In half an hour he restored my authority with the soldiers. I have never met anyone like him. The whole time, out in the yard during my interior rehabilitation and while I was in the tub, his mouth was set in a stern and bitter line. But his large, wine-shiny eyes transmitted a different message: he was highly amused.

Bagamoyo

18 March

Three days from now we'll leave Bagamoyo. The last few days have allowed me to regain my balance, thank God. The absence of any remarkable event and the unvarying routine have agreed well with me. Even my stomach has performed satisfactorily. But now my anxiety is returning: there's pressure in my chest and an unpleasant itch under my skin. My stomach is acting up too, but Stanley says that's part of life in the tropics.

"Just let the shit fly," he says impishly.

I wish I were back at sea.

It's evening now, and I can see the soldiers' campfires from my window. I have grown accustomed to their chatter and laughter—it even makes me feel at home. In spite of their superstitiousness and their fear of the dark, Negroes have an amazing ability to make themselves at home in it. They huddle around their fires and their voices assume a darker sound. I sense a deep and mysterious undercurrent in their nocturnal conversations.

The soldiers no longer make fun of me. They have simply tired of me and concentrate on adjusting to life here in Bagamoyo. They spend a great deal of time skulking about looking for women, and many of them have started bartering with the villagers. There have been a few disputes between soldiers and villagers over some woman or commodity, but none of them have been serious. The arguments are easily resolved as soon as Stanley picks up the big donkey whip.

Tonight the sea breeze has stayed out at sea. The air is motionless in my small room. Drops of sweat run down my arms, make ugly stains on the paper, blur the ink. The donkeys and the two horses in the corral are restless tonight, perhaps because of the heat. They stamp about and seem irritated. Or do they have a premonition of our departure? They say animals have a sixth sense. I'll go and chat to them soothingly before I turn in.

Strange how Africa can sometimes feel so much like home. I've noticed this the last couple of days here in Bagamoyo, as I sometimes noticed it in Zanzibar or various ports I've been stuck in for a few weeks when a ship was delayed. But this feeling-at-home has always seemed connected with uneventfulness. As soon as I am forced to undertake something, to move, to watch others working, I become dispirited. My body feels heavy and awkward. Yet there is always a sense of panic hovering below these comfortable quiet times, the dark background of happiness, and that is why I always find myself on the run again—to my own surprise.

The day after I recovered from my fever, Stanley and Farquhar set me to serious work. We had to sew tents out of waterproof sailcloth, for shelter in the rainy season. It was truly hard and boring work. The strong hempen cloth was difficult to handle, but I felt quite comfortable with Farquhar, sullen as he was. We sat in the shade of a mango tree and sewed away, exchanging occasional words about the expedition or events in camp. Since the labor was monotonous and there wasn't much drama in Bagamoyo (*we* were the dramatic element), we didn't have much to say. Once in a while Farquhar would offer me a drink—who knows where he got the stuff. Probably cadged it off Stanley.

By and large, Stanley left us alone. He had a sufficiency of other worries: only his regular morning swim in the ocean prevented him from riddling the local business people with bullets, or so he claimed. One morning I followed him surreptitiously, to observe this ritual. Ramrod-straight, with strides too long for his legs, he proceeded down to the beach on a sandy path, accompanied by Selim. On the beach, he took off his clothes slowly and ceremoniously, handing them to Selim, who folded them into a tidy pile. Selim's responsibilities included keeping any spectators at a respectful distance.

From my vantage point behind a sturdy palm trunk I was surprised to see that he stripped down completely before putting on his bathing costume. His body was slighter and more boyish than I had imagined. He had neither the bulk and weight nor the well-developed musculature of a full-grown man. It seemed almost indecent when that frail, fair-skinned, hairless body slowly entered the sea. He went out a long way, to struggle with the tremendous surf. Sometimes his head disappeared, only to bob up again in the eddies. I was almost afraid for his sake. Selim stood looking the other way, as if embarrassed by what was taking place in the water.

Later that day Stanley said to me:

"I saw you were interested in my morning swim. You should try it yourself. Do you a power of good."

It's a mystery to me how he was able to detect me behind that palm tree. He must have his spies.

Business matters have been weighing on his mind. I don't envy him. At first he entered into negotiations with an Arab who promised to find him the porters he needed. After receiving his earnest money, that fellow promptly vanished. Next Stanley turned to a remarkable young Indian who had been recommended to him by a successful businessman in Zanzibar. It was this excellent youth, Soor Hadji Palloo, brave, indefatigable, and cunning as an international financier, whom Stanley would have liked to use for target practice one day. Nevertheless, he showed amazing patience with the boy. It might be said that he was simply compelled to do so, having realized that his only hope of acquiring a sufficient number of porters lay with this stripling.

One morning Farquhar and I witnessed a discussion between Stanley and the young Hindu in Stanley's dining room. Farquhar, animated for a change, had been arguing with Stanley about the wisdom of taking horses into the interior. Farquhar very rarely argues with anybody, but now he was insistent: horses weren't able to survive in the African interior, he had it on many good authorities. Stanley pooh-poohed this claim and pointed out that zebras seemed to be doing quite well in the very heart of the continent!

Just then a small, frail figure appeared in the doorway. Because of his light skin and nice clothes, I thought he was an emissary of one of the wealthy Arabs. Stanley immediately broke off the conversation with Farquhar and bade the youth enter. The latter quickly removed his shoes and rushed into the room with many little bows. Stanley offered him a seat, but he explained, in a curiously top-heavy English that seemed to roll around in his mouth, that he was not worthy to sit down with white men. On the other hand, he seemed to feel free to roam around the room. As he passed me, I felt his fingertips on my cotton shirt and winced as if I'd been accosted by a pickpocket. He could not resist fingering Stanley's whip and shirt sleeve, whereupon Stanley swiped at his hand the way one would swat a mosquito. Fat Farquhar sidestepped the spiderlike newcomer with a lopsided grin, but the boy caught up with him in a corner and got a pinch of the khaki material covering Farquhar's rear.

I had never observed anything quite so farcical. While this Soor Hadji Palloo took possession of the room by examining the quality of every piece of fabric and every single object, he kept up an incessant patter and performed his little bows in this direction and that. Stanley's face took on a darker coloration.

"Stand still, goddamn it!" he shouted. The youth came to a halt and bowed.

The only sound in the room was the smacking he produced as he stood there smiling and chewing betel nuts or God knows what.

After a while, Stanley persuaded him to give a step-by-step report on his efforts to procure porters. The transactions were of such a complicated nature that they surpassed my understanding. To tell the truth, I don't think Stanley really understood them either. This much I could follow: the bales of fabric and the beads, which represented the price of the porters and Palloo's commission, were now in the young Hindu's hands—or, more likely, spread among his enormous network of business contacts. Thus, Palloo had the goods, but Stanley did not yet have a single porter.

Stanley demanded explanations, appealed to the Hindu's business ethics, accused him of reneging on promises, and finally threatened to have him flayed alive. Palloo weathered it all and dished up further dizzying explanations as to why he had such problems providing the porters on time. He could come up with slaves at a day's notice, but free caravan porters were harder to find.

Stanley was racing against time, he wanted to be under way. Palloo, on the other hand, regarded time as his most reliable accomplice.

I took a liking to the young Hindu. Nothing fazed him, and he was smarter than anyone else around. Stanley was trying to bully his way through the labyrinthine business transactions by a display of power, but that was just like trying to destroy an anthill with a rifle shot. Stanley simply does not understand business matters, and Palloo surely regards him as an uncivilized roughneck who uses force instead of cunning. It is amusing that I consider Palloo more civilized than Stanley. Perhaps I have become a barbarian?

Palloo noticed immediately that I found the palaver entertaining. He winked at me in an impudent and conspiratorial fashion, and asked in a whisper whether I was interested in doing some private business with him. The next day he sent me a rooster as a present, and every time I ran into him—always trotting to or from Stanley and always in a good mood—he would give a little laugh and bow several times without breaking stride. Never before had I met a person who managed to be insolent and humble at the same time.

Now, at last, Stanley has all his porters. However, he did not come out ahead on the deal; he was too impatient.

As long as four weeks ago he sent off the first caravan—he has divided the expedition into five caravans, in order to make it more mobile and less vulnerable to attack. If one of them is wiped out, the other four remain. The first contingent was made up of twenty-four porters and three soldiers. The second, which left a few days later, consisted of twenty-eight porters, two subalterns, and two soldiers. The third was under the command of none other than earnest Farquhar, and it left another few days later, at the end of February. He was accompanied by twenty-two porters, a cook, three soldiers, and ten donkeys.

I must admit that it pained me to see Farquhar disappear down the caravan route as the only white man in his group. I can't say we had become great friends, but we had become accustomed to one another, and I had felt safe sitting and sewing canvas with him. When the road had swallowed up his caravan, I felt lonely and abandoned.

"God bless you, Shaw, should we not meet again" were his last words to me, in typical bird-of-ill-omen fashion.

Who is going to look after me now if I'm stricken by illness? Not Stanley. I wonder if Farquhar wasn't a little proud to have been given the solitary command of a caravan—to be the expedition's first white man to penetrate unexplored territory. Still, he looked mostly depressed as the small donkey's stiff, jerky legs carried his heavy frame away toward the unknown.

The fourth caravan left Bagamoyo on the eleventh of March with fifty-five porters, two subalterns, and three soldiers. We'll be leaving in three days' time, as the fifth and final caravan. According to Stanley's plan—after Farquhar left, I was assigned the paperwork for the expedition—it will be composed of Stanley and myself, twenty-eight porters, twelve soldiers, a tailor (Arab), a cook (Arab), an interpreter (Arab), a rifle-bearer, seventeen donkeys, two horses, and a dog. The entire expedition consists of 192 men. It can hardly be said that we're proceeding to the interior in an inconspicuous fashion.

As I sit here writing, a monotonous drumbeat begins. The curious thing is that I've never seen anyone beating a drum here in Africa, even though I have heard the sound countless times. I associate it with jungles growing down to endless sandy beaches like a tangled wall, or with vast plains stretching out to the ocean like an enormous tongue. The drumbeat seems to be coming from every direction at once. There is a fever in the pulsing rhythm, a madness that frightens me. Just now, I can't place the sound: is it the soldiers and bearers outside who are drumming, or is it people on the far side of Bagamoyo, or is it coming from a neighboring village? I can't tell. The sound is simply there, another constituent of the night's darkness.

My writing was interrupted by little Saburi. I gave a start when he cleared his throat in the doorway; I hadn't heard anyone coming. He bowed and held his palms together in a gentle gesture. Then he pulled something out of a ragged trouser pocket and held it out to me: a small, knobbly object. Looking down at the floor, he mumbled:

"Gift. Protection on trip."

At first I was apprehensive and thought he wanted to poison me by some native magic. I pointed at the table, and he carefully placed the little parcel next to my papers.

"Hide!"

"Why are you giving me this?" I asked.

He didn't understand, just shook his head. Language will be my bane on our march. I don't have any Swahili—just a few words—and the porters and soldiers know only a few phrases of English. Stanley, of course, has Selim, who is with him constantly, serves him, and acts as his interpreter. I don't have anybody like that.

Was it revenge Saburi was after? Did he want to cast a spell on me with this dirty fetish, or whatever it was? While I sat there brooding, staring at the object, I heard someone cough outside my room. The sound was clearly audible through the pulsing of the drums. Startled, I pointed at the door and asked:

"Who is it?"

Asmani's big grinning face appeared in the doorway. He salaamed; God knows what he was grinning about. He came in and stood beside his little comrade. At once the room felt crowded. Asmani was tremendously well built, and his physique indicated both strength and speed. The only disharmonious aspect of this apparition of divine unspoiled nature was his squeaky voice. Little Saburi had been blessed with the deep and resonant organ that would have accorded well with Asmani's citadel of muscle.

But what did they want from me? As my first fright abated, curiosity drew my fingers to the object on the table. Cautiously I picked it up, unfolded a few leaves that had been cleverly woven into a protective cover, and pulled out a small wooden doll—or idol, I should say. It was a carving of a female figure, pregnant, with a big smooth belly. It was beautiful in its own way, and there was something childlike and touching about it.

"Thank you."

I felt a bit embarrassed, and a bit moved as well. Both their faces brightened when they saw that their gift had been accepted, and they bowed and turned to leave. In my relief that nothing worse had happened, I had an inspiration.

"Wait!"

They halted and turned as I pulled two coils of metal wire out of my trunk. Farquhar had advised me to bring a small trove of personal gifts. I held them out. Asmani laughed, slowly and thoughtfully, to confirm that both gift and counter-gift had functioned in a satisfactory manner.

"Friends!" Saburi said emphatically, and pointed at

the three of us. I nodded in response, and they were gone into the night.

After they had left, I sat lost in thought for a while, holding the little figure. Why did they want to make friends with me? Or was it all a hypocritical ruse whose true intent was to hurt me? Had Farquhar been there, I would have asked him. But for the faintly sour odor the two Negroes had left behind, I would have doubted that they had been there at all.

The voices outside have been silenced, the fires are down to glowing coals. Now the drums and the crickets rule the night. Soon I'll go to bed, although it is too warm for easy sleep. The night breeze is still lingering out at sea. Damp, stifling heat has piled up in my room, layer upon layer.

Night is a difficult time. I wonder how she is doing in the half-breed's house. I hope the goddamn crook isn't mistreating her. I don't understand why I'm still thinking about her.

Is it truly my fate to follow this expedition into the deepest darkness? Why is my life changing tack? I'm almost forty now and ought to be set in my ways. Did Stanley pick me by accident, or was I meant for some purpose? Do I have a task to accomplish? It seems all my thoughts are questions these days. As a sailor, I've always believed that you can feel closest to the mysteries of life out at sea, when you stand looking down into the continuously changing motion of the water. Here I feel as if I weren't inside my own body—as if Stanley had just happened to lend me some muscles and blood so I could follow him.

I think about that first bite of Christmas apple, about

the feeling you get walking out on a cold and happy winter's day when your breath stands like smoke in the air and frozen puddles crackle under your boots. Will I ever experience that again?

I also think of a day many years ago, out at sea. Our ship was suddenly surrounded by huge baleen whales. Their slow, lazy movements in the cold water were like an omen. Good or bad? Everybody on board laid down their work, and the entire crew lined the rails, reverently watching those enormous creatures. There was something touching about them precisely because they were so large, so silent, and so many. They came from another world. I particularly remember the almost imperceptible motion of the ship when one of them softly butted and rubbed against its starboard side. They led a dignified life. Will I ever again see a whale? I have to be content with the small female figurine. I think that in some strange fashion it has caused me to remember the whales.

I don't intend to write anything further here in Bagamoyo. The next time I pick up my pen I may know a little more about what it means to journey into the heart of Africa.

Simbamwenni

19 April 1871

I am in a fairy-tale town. Simbamwenni, the "Lion City," is like a legend, a fantasia of the Orient and the tropics. Yet it really exists, here in the shadow of the Uruguru Mountains in the flowering Ungerengeri Valley, where the sky pours down its waters and then the sun comes out to burn in a bright blue sky. Here, both sun and moon cast their light on a proud and beautiful people. I feel fortunate—fortunate but ugly. The more glorious the people appear in their nakedness, the more unkempt, sweaty, and awkward I feel.

Simbamwenni—the name itself has an opulent ring. This place will be as decisive for me as Kingaru was, but in a wholly different way.

When we approached the city and first saw the stockade girding the hundreds of huts on the far side of the river, the porters and soldiers sang out, in unison, "Simbamwenni, Simbamwenni, the Lion City, mightiest of all." A stream of people poured from the foursquare fortifications: it was like poking an anthill with a stick. They were all carrying bows, spears, or firearms, but their advance did not seem threatening in the least. They were laughing and shouting to us from the far side of the mighty river. Our arrival seemed to please them.

But I am getting ahead of myself. Before we reached this legendary city, we were compelled—as always in fairy tales—to pass by the gates of hell first. It is questionable whether we didn't, in fact, pass through them.

We left Bagamoyo on the twenty-first of March. Reveille was before sunup: true, all preparations had been completed on the previous day, but Stanley was impatient and wanted to get going as early as possible. He was excited, like a child with travel fever; roses flamed on his cheeks, and he kept rushing about among the soldiers and porters, shouting terse orders.

By the time dawn came, damp and cool, people had assembled at our camp to witness the departure. The horses and donkeys were restless and noisy. The porters and soldiers, on the other hand, stood calmly at ease and watched Stanley with amusement as he bustled about the camp.

At nine o'clock we were ready to march. The first man to start out was our guide, Hamadi, an experienced and fearless caravan leader of whom it was said that he had a woman in every village between Bagamoyo and Ujiji. He had also been assigned the task of carrying the American flag, which he accepted reluctantly from his master. During most of the march he carried it on his shoulder, rolled up. Now and again, especially when we were approaching inhabited regions, Stanley ordered him to unfurl it.

After Hamadi came Stanley on his bay horse, straight-backed as a general, his head pulled heavenward by an invisible force. Then came the soldiers in charge of the pack train of donkeys. Young Selim had been given command of a donkey cart that Stanley insisted on taking along. Then came all the porters and, bringing up the rear, myself. I wasn't too pleased about being the "overseer," as Stanley called it. During the march I had the constant feeling that someone was stalking me, watching me from behind.

Our departure was impressive. The porters and soldiers raised their voices in song, the spectators yelled and waved, there was life and commotion, and everybody seemed happy. With a sweeping wave of his arm and a shrill shout, Stanley sent the caravan on its way. Hamadi, who plodded along between dense rows of spectators and tall mimosa hedges, couldn't help performing monkey tricks and making obscene gestures for the benefit of the beauties of Bagamoyo. But Stanley made up for him in seriousness.

It still took almost ten minutes before the rear of the column began to move. The donkey I was mounted on just stood there looking stubborn, hanging its head. When it finally received the order to go from the heels of my kicking feet, it started off in its jerky fashion. This was my first time on a donkey's back, and my initial thought was that the beast wasn't really suited for riding. You sat too close to the ground and took a severe, erratic buffeting. It was like straddling a bullock or a large boar, some animal with too small a body and a mercurial temper.

I had just crossed the large open yard that had been our campground for many weeks when the caravan halted. The porters in front of me flung their burdens to the ground and burst into raucous laughter. That African laughter, so incomprehensible to me! No one was able to interpret. Some teenage boys came up to me and started pulling at my clothes and gear. I tried to shoo them off, but they showed no respect.

Then Stanley returned at full gallop, and the spectators scattered. He reined in his horse right in front of my startled mount.

"All the donkeys have broken loose and stampeded into a manioc field. Come on, help us round them up again!"

He vanished in a cloud of dust. I urged my little donkey on but it didn't succeed in outdistancing the boys, who trotted alongside and went on pestering me. I passed the long row of cheerful porters, all of whom had settled down comfortably atop their burdens. As soon as I arrived at the edge of the manioc field, my donkey pricked up its huge ears and uttered a terrible bray that made its stomach muscles contract spasmodically between my legs. The cry met with a many-voiced response from the middle of the field, and my donkey lost every grain of sense it may ever have had. It charged off full tilt, leaving the road and invading the field. I needed all my strength to hang on to the saddle. When my steed reached its comrades, many of which were now lying on the ground, having lost their balance under their heavy loads, it came to a sudden halt, and I managed to stay on only by grabbing its ears. Stanley and a few soldiers were busy prodding some of the creatures back to their feet.

"Good show, Shaw! Full speed ahead, what?" Stanley shouted to me in his shrill voice.

In half an hour we were back on the road. It was a liberating feeling, like coming to a decision after long hesitation.

So this was Africa. I was surprised to find the country beyond Bagamoyo so fertile and so densely populated. All along the caravan route we saw naked Negroes working in the fields. Most of them pointed at me and laughed. I had expected only savannahs, forests, and savages sustaining themselves by hunting and gathering berries, fruits, and roots. But here, scattered across these undulating plains stretching down to the sea in long dunes, were fields of manioc, maize, bananas, and sugarcane, pepper plantations, et cetera. The road wound up and down, along waterways and stands of thick, tangled jungle. During the first days we also traversed a large forest area with many kinds of antelope and monkeys. Stanley, always eager for the hunt, returned from his escapades in that dense forest torn and tattered and all but empty-handed. He can never set eyes on a wild beast without blasting away. The soldiers laughed behind his back.

The forest inspires respect. When I go into it to relieve myself, I often come back with bad scrapes and scratches. The variety of species is tremendous. I can't name a single bird or tree. There are three kinds of tree I have learned to recognize, but they're not trees of the jungle. The first is the mango, which grows around villages and along the caravan route. It is a tree for man, providing a great deal of fruit and shade. It is also a resting place for slave caravans, and in its shelter there is lively commerce, resolution of disputes, and announcement of verdicts. It is a tree that presides over laments as well as laughter.

The second is a tree of the savannah, the plains, open country: the acacia. It is a tree for wild beasts. Untouched by man, it seems almost to float, ready to ascend to heaven. It gives shade to animals and hunters and is probably most beautiful when seen at a distance.

The third is the king of trees, the baobab. It always stands alone, here and there, without apparent reason, and it is usually very old. In its weight and dignity it resembles the oaks of Europe. In its branches live owls and other birds, and the thirsty traveler may find rain-water in its cavities. A couple of days ago when we made a brief halt by a baobab, Selim told us Africans believe that God has turned the baobab upside down, pointing its roots at the sky. Selim said the Creator wanted to punish the tree for its arrogance by hiding its beautiful crown underground. Thus, no one has ever seen the full foliage of a baobab.

Otherwise, I know nothing about the country we are penetrating, nothing about the people. Can't distinguish them (Swahili, Hehe, Kimbu, Nyamwezi?), don't know any of their languages, not even Swahili. But does Stanley know any more? True, he asks many questions, and I try to catch Selim's replies whenever I happen to be within earshot. Yet I sometimes get the feeling that Stanley doesn't listen to the answers he receives.

It is hard to describe my feeling for this land. I often find myself curiously devoid of thoughts and emotions. These plains and forests put me into a trancelike state of rest, an emptiness that is almost euphoric. But then, for no reason at all, that passive state of bliss may change into a sense of loneliness and futility. Nature is so incomprehensibly vast that I want to die. There is in the landscape a sorrow as profound as the one that overtakes you when you return, as a grownup, to the scenes of your childhood and realize that it's all over. Paradoxically, it seems as if time has stopped and is now flowing through your body without meeting any resistance. During our expedition I've often had the sensation that something significant has just taken place but we have arrived too late. There are moods here that resemble those you may experience in the middle of an ocean on calm days—the only difference being that over savannah and acacia there lies a more somber melancholy, one implicated with deep-seated memories. Above the ocean lies only total oblivion.

Little Saburi, who already looks weary of marching, even though as a soldier he only carries his rifle and a small bundle, sat down next to me when we stopped for a rest. He started talking in his halting English—where did he learn it? Confused thoughts tumbled out of his mouth, each word illustrated with small but decisive gestures. I remember exactly what he said.

"One day, the birds will fall to the ground. The rivers will stop running, and two suns will rise in the sky, one from the east and one from the west. Just as they meet in the sky—"

Then he fell silent, clenched his small hands into fists, and shook them in the air. After a while he asked me where I kept the female figurine he'd given me. When I pointed at one of my trunks, he smiled contentedly, got up, and joined the other soldiers.

The march itself is terrible. Riding on the donkey gives me a nagging back pain; my kidneys and buttocks go numb, and so do my feet. At the rest stops, sitting down does not provide any real relief for my back and legs, and my feet become even more swollen and clogged with blood. To spare myself those pains in my back, I have even tried walking next to the donkey, but the simple truth is that I am not fit to march on foot. On the uphill stretches I pant like a dog, and my eyes smart from huge drops of salty sweat that pour down my forehead and blind me. My shirt sticks to me uncomfortably and is as wet as if I had washed it.

Every minute I am aware of the muscles, tendons, fluids, and nerves in my body. I am not cut out for this life. When I see how the porters stride up tremendous inclines carrying fifty pounds on their heads, I fully realize what different creatures Negroes are.

Despite all that, it was bearable—until we reached Kingaru. There, the physical torment gnawed its way into far more vulnerable parts of my body. The very name of the place nauseates me. The village lies in a deep canyon with steep walls covered by a dark, thick forest that smells exactly like rotten meat. Just as we were descending into the trees, the sky grew alarmingly dark. The porters looked up at the dense foliage above us and shouted *masika* to each other; the rainy season had begun.

I had uneasy premonitions even before we entered the village. This was not the Africa I had encountered just past Bagamoyo. These were not undulating plains in white sunshine, or dense jungles dripping with water and rich odors; this was not the mild dark of the night with cool breezes, nor was it moonlight with wild beasts howling (jackals, hyenas, lions?), their cries echoing off blue-black mountain ridges. Here was silence and stench. The very place exuded death and cruelty, cunning, malice, ugliness. How people could have chosen to live in this unhealthy pit, this arsehole of a diarrhetic, was incomprehensible. They must be the Devil's kin.

As we arrived in the village, the black clouds released an ocean. I have never seen such rain. It hurt when it struck the unclothed body. In a few seconds, before the porters had time to set down their loads, the water was streaming between the huts and dissolving the hard-packed soil into one gigantic mud puddle. In this mire we were to pitch our tents and prepare for the night. Paralyzed by the horror of it, I sank down next to a tree trunk that provided some cover. The powerful rain pounded down into the running water and created clouds of mist that obscured everything beyond a couple of yards.

My faintness increased. I was ready to burst into tears.

Right in the middle of the cloudburst I caught a glimpse of Stanley's white jacket. He was beating and whipping the porters, driving them into the huts, where they evicted whole families so that our cargo could be secured under the roofs. Everything that didn't fit into the huts was piled up under a few big mango trees. That done, he ordered the porters and soldiers to pitch the tents. As if in a dream, I watched how they slid and staggered in the mud, trying to get those tents up in the storm.

Then Stanley spotted me.

"Shaw! You lazy swine!"

I had to lend a hand. It makes me tired just to think about it. I was exhausted and kept falling down in the mud and water. I can't remember how long I lasted.

Just before dusk, the rain stopped. It was followed by an unpleasant silence, broken only by the helpless bleating of the odd goat and, from a thicket, the weeping of babies forced from their huts. Heavy drops fell from the trees and made a plopping sound when they hit the puddles.

Stanley summoned me. The chief of the village was paying a visit, and for some reason Stanley wanted me there.

"You have to learn how to pay tribute. You have to guard against getting cheated."

A few minutes later we were joined by a toothless old man who stank of urine and the sweat of a lifetime. This was the chief, accompanied by a few younger men. His lips were drawn in a grotesque grin, and his eyes gleamed with greed and curiosity. The customary gift from these chiefs was a goat, a couple of chickens, or a prepared banquet for several people. Stanley's tribute often consisted of fabric. Although the chiefs' gifts were never evaluated, the counter-gift, the tribute, was frequently the subject of long negotiations.

Kingaru's wizened little chief held out a small bowl of rice to Stanley, who stared down at it with an awkward expression. Then Stanley laughed, pulled out a tiny bit of fabric, and nonchalantly tossed it to the chief. The latter let his jaw hang down in astonishment, then mumbled excitedly:

"This is no gift. This is much too small."

"If you call that bowl of rice a gift, that piece of fabric is a gift too."

"This is a poor village."

"If you wish to receive a valuable tribute, you have to give a valuable gift. You can go now."

Selim, who had acted as interpreter during this exchange, seemed embarrassed, and Bombay, who had been listening, shook his craggy head. He looked worried. Stanley was cheerful, calm, and resolute.

As soon as the disappointed chief left, Stanley took me to the corral. His mood changed within the minute. His spare horse, the apple of his eye, a white one he'd been given by the Sultan of Zanzibar, had shown symptoms of disease. Now it stood there hanging its head, foam around its mouth. It had had difficulty walking the last stretch to Kingaru. Stanley felt its hot muzzle and gulped.

"Well, Farquhar warned you—"

That was as much as I managed to say before he struck me across the mouth.

"To hell with Farquhar! To hell with you, and to hell with the horses, the donkeys, the porters, the soldiers! If need be, I'll get to Ujiji on my own! But no one is permitted to give up! You either obey me or you die. There are no other alternatives. From now on, anyone who disobeys me will be flogged or shot!"

"That'll use up a lot of ammunition."

He stared like a madman; his face turned linen-white, his hands shook, his chin trembled, and he seemed about to burst into tears. Then something broke the stare, and for the first time I saw him blink. He swayed and had to lean on the enfeebled horse. From his mouth came noises that sounded like sobs.

Just as he seemed to be on the very edge of collapse, a shudder passed through his body. He straightened up and bit his bloodless lips until the color returned. In a whisper—it had grown dark around us—he said:

"Shaw—I shall stop at nothing. *Nothing*. I shall find

56

the light of Africa. The light that shineth in the darkness."

He gave me a quick glance out of the corner of his eye, as if ashamed of this sentimental twaddle. I saw the white of that eye flash in the dark. Then he stared straight out into the night—not blinking.

While I thought he was being ridiculous with his balderdash about light and darkness, I was impressed by the incredible strength and determination that radiated from him, as tangibly as heat radiates from a fire. There in the dark, beside the dying horse, I understood better than ever that he was indeed made of different stuff. I would never have survived the onslaught that had been shaking him a few moments ago.

The following morning I woke up feeling like I was trapped inside the body of a huge beast. The air was close, the sky overcast and gray. Pressure and humidity made my head hurt. My tent was a stomach whose powerful acids were about to dissolve my body. Drops of condensation hung from the canvas ceiling.

I stepped outside to urinate, but the claustrophobic feeling didn't go away. It was dawn; everything was sketched in pencil, everything tasted of ashes. Only now I noticed that my tent stood a little apart from the others, on a slope on the outskirts of the village. During my awkward attempts to pitch it I must have moved away from the others.

With a nagging physical sense of discomfort, I sat down just inside the open flap of the tent, with a view of a small forest clearing where a path ran down into a dell. The path probably led to a spring or creek. As I was sitting there, an adolescent girl came into sight. I watched her back as she slowly made her way down the path, balancing a jar on her head. She walked with a limp.

A moment later, I heard stealthy steps approaching, and two of our soldiers appeared. I recognized them but didn't know their names. Neither the girl nor the men had seen me sitting in the darkness of the tent. Silently they followed her down the path. When she noticed them she stopped, perturbed. She seemed afraid to run into the forest, afraid to turn around on the path. The men approached her slowly, talking to her in low, soothing voices. She didn't utter a sound.

Finally she took a couple of limping steps and tried to get past them, but they had no trouble catching her. As they grabbed her she cried out but was quickly silenced by a hand over her mouth. It sounded like the brief cry of a forest bird. Quickly and efficiently they dragged her behind a clump of bushes. I could only catch glimpses of them now, but the bigger of the two flung himself upon her first, while the other one squatted and held her. After a few seconds they exchanged places, and then it was all over. The act itself didn't take more than a minute. These were experienced rapists who did not torment their victims gratuitously.

As they came back up the slope, one of the soldiers held something out to her, but she sniffled and shook her head. Walking fast now, the men returned to the village, and she limped along behind them. She had forgotten her jar. Her sniffles turned into weeping, and she crumpled to the ground with a doleful cry. An old woman saw her and came scurrying down the path.

I crawled deeper into my tent, into hiding. My heart was beating violently. What had happened? Why hadn't I intervened? It was like one of those nightmares where you find yourself watching something abominable but are unable to act because your arms and legs won't function.

A rape, first thing in the morning, out in the open, just a stone's throw from our camp.

I peeked out again. Maybe I had imagined it all. But the old woman had put her arm around the girl and was leading her away, and other women were gathering.

An image of my girl in Zanzibar superimposed itself on the scene. The half-breed, grinning.

I got up resolutely and went straight to Stanley. His unbending sense of justice would strike the culprits down. When I entered his tent, still full of resolve, he looked at me in surprise. Selim was just serving him tea.

"Good morning! Sir, I have just witnessed a rape, and I demand that the perpetrators be punished. They should be executed, as an example to the others!"

He glanced down at his teacup. Tonelessly, he said: "That horse. It died."

"I can point out the two soldiers who did it."

"I said the horse died! Listen, if I started meddling in all their love affairs—"

"But this was rape!"

"Why didn't you do something then?"

"There wasn't time!"

He laughed.

"Well, why don't you arrest and court-martial them yourself? You have my authorization to do so. The only thing I ask is that you hire two new soldiers of comparable competence to replace them."

If I hadn't felt faint and dizzy at that moment, I would have punched him. I had hardly had time to think through his reply when he pulled me out of the tent to go see the dead horse. Now there were people standing in front of every hut, watching us in silence. I noticed that many were disfigured by leprosy and smallpox. They would have killed us if they could.

Half of the horse carcass lay under a big bush. It looked as if the creature had tried to hide when its hour came. Bombay, dark and silent, stood guard, the hulking Asmani by his side. Stanley ordered them to pull the horse forward. It slid easily in the mud, its legs stretched out rigidly.

"Cut it open."

"It get sick and die. Why not leave?" Bombay protested in a low voice.

"Cut it open!"

Asmani stepped up, placed his left foot on the horse's flank, and plunged a knife into its abdomen. With a few powerful strokes he cut it open, and stomach and intestines spilled onto the ground, the guts writhing like snakes. When he sliced into a piece of intestine, a mass of long white worms tumbled out. The stomach, too, was full of them. I turned away. I felt as if those worms were crawling in my own gullet.

"Other horse sick too," Bombay observed dryly, and pointed to the far end of the *boma,* as the corral was called. There, the bay horse stood hanging its head a small distance from the donkeys, which seemed to want to avoid their dying cousin.

Stanley licked his lips nervously and stomped around in the mud, stared at the horse, stared at the worms at his feet. He rapped the side of his boot with the whip. The rain was starting up again.

"Shoot the other one, and bury them both. Take ten men. The others will break camp. We're leaving in three hours."

"Not possible," said Bombay. "Half men sick. Diarrhea. Fever. Take couple days leave Kingaru."

"Well, carry on and bury those beasts in any case."

Stanley's voice broke, and he hurried off to his tent. Asmani gave a sad little laugh, but Bombay looked sullen and shook his head.

It took a few soldiers all day to dig a hole sufficiently large to accommodate both horses. The villagers became restless. The young men ran in and out of the chief's hut while the women and children contented themselves with staring at us out of dark eyes. In the afternoon a message came from the chief, informing Stanley that he and the chiefs of a great number of neighboring villages had decided to impose a fine on the white man for burying horses, without permission, in the ground of their fathers.

This got Stanley back on his feet. He became lively and pugnacious. He replied curtly that if the chief had anything to say to him, he should do so in person. A few hours later the chief appeared in front of Stanley's tent and was admitted immediately. He had with him two young men of impressive physique, armed with spears. In addition to Stanley and myself, Bombay and a feverish Selim were present. The chief began his speech.

"To bury dead horses in the ground of our fathers is a great crime. The spirits of our fathers will punish all of us. The only thing we can do to placate them is to offer them gift. As chief of Kingaru, I sentence you to pay a fine of two dotis of fabric, because this is a grave transgression."

The small, foul-smelling old man was shaking with indignation. The solemnity of the occasion seemed to have returned some of his former authority to him. The honor and welfare of his village rested on his shrunken shoulders.

Smiling, Stanley rose to his feet, walked over to the chief, and asked him sarcastically:

"Are you a great chief?"

"I am chief of Kingaru and all its surroundings."

"How many soldiers do you have?"

The old man's indignation began to fade, replaced by curiosity and suspicion.

"Answer me."

"I have none."

Stanley laughed out loud and shook the chief by his shoulders.

"And yet you come here and demand two dotis of fabric from a wealthy and mighty man who has many soldiers armed with rifles. How do you propose to take them from me?"

"Not take them. You will give them away, to placate the spirits of the fathers. If you do not, great misfortune will befall both you and us. My verdict has been in your interest as well as ours."

"No one tells me what is in my interest!"

Bombay said in a gruff voice:

"Arabs would pay. Ivory hunter, slave trader. All pay."

For a moment, there was silence in the tent. Stanley drifted off for a few seconds and just stared at Bombay. Suddenly his face brightened, and he ordered Bombay to have the horses dug up again and let them lie where they had expired. Then the whole village would run the danger of contamination from the rotting carcasses.

After Selim, still feverish, had translated this, the chief became incredibly agitated. The situation had taken a turn he had not foreseen, and he no longer knew how to handle it. All the authority trickled out of the poor old fellow. He turned and reeled out of the tent, followed by the grim bodyguards. Outside, he stopped, turned back, and weakly begged Stanley to leave the horses buried. Then, in a quavery voice, shaking his arms at the sky, he said something Selim did not translate. It sounded like a curse.

Stanley laughed out loud.

As I came out of the tent, I ran into Saburi, the runt, who had watched the chief's retreat with disquiet in his gaze. "Terrible, terrible," he muttered to me.

I pushed him out of the way and went to my tent. He disgusted me, that little bird of ill omen. Since we left Bagamoyo I had found out that the other soldiers and porters avoided him, treating him with a combination of hostility, respect, and revulsion. Asmani alone accepted his company. The hand I had used to shove him aside felt unclean.

I missed, and still miss, Farquhar. He may be the only one on this expedition who is in his right mind. Perhaps Bombay is too, as thuggish as he looks.

That night I slept fitfully and was plagued by nightmares. I dreamed that I was sitting in the kitchen of my childhood home, in the company of my father. The kitchen was much smaller than it had really been, and it was frightfully cold. Although I had all my clothes on, I was so cold I was shaking. Mother stood in a corner,

Father sat at the end of the kitchen table. His enormous body filled up half the room. The plates in front of us were crawling with worms, and he was shoveling them into his mouth with great appetite. He forced me to eat them as well. As I swallowed, my whole body turned red-hot, and I broke out in a sweat. Mother just stood in the corner and cried.

When I woke up, I was drenched in sweat and felt violently ill. I staggered to my feet and out into the dark. It was drizzling. Before I got my trousers down, my rear end exploded. While I was struggling out of the soiled garment, I slipped in the mud and sat down in the unspeakable muck. Filthy and streaked with my own loose excrement, I crawled back into the tent and lay there for several days. I didn't come out until the day we got under way again.

Saburi looked after me as if I were a sick child. If he hadn't, I would have died. He gave me water and cleaned me up. I was too weak even to get up to relieve myself. Saburi wiped me off and took care of everything. I spent my time staring at the canvas walls or lying in a sleepy torpor. I didn't care whether it was day or night. It felt as if I had been devoured whole by a large animal. The sounds of the village and camp were remote. My nostrils were permeated by the odor of excreta and decay.

Saburi placed the small pregnant figurine right next to my head. I let it stand there until I started imagining that it was growing and giving me nightmares. I pushed it away then, but after a little while it was back where it had been.

Not once did Stanley come to visit me. Not an hour passed when I did not long for him to do so.

Simbamwenni

21 April

Stanley has received his comeuppance for our recent altercation—about which more later. Well, whether that's so or not, the fact is that he became ill yesterday, for the first time, and behaved as miserably as any spoiled woman. Selim sat on the edge of his bed, wiped his brow, kept him company, and generally took care of him. He even sang songs to him. Stanley does not like visitors when he is indisposed; and so I invented several errands to his tent.

The first time I went he was lying there in a delirium, holding Selim's hand. The next time he had perked up a bit and was sufficiently conscious to vent his irritation on his faithful servant, who had to perform the most demeaning tasks. I don't understand Stanley. Sometimes one might think that Selim is his son. For instance: when Selim became ill in Kingaru, he was given permission to rest in Stanley's bed, which caused even stone-faced Bombay to register surprise. Stanley is capable of boxing Selim's ears in front of porters and soldiers, and then, the very next moment, putting his arm around his shoulders and walking him over to the tent, engrossed in intimate conversation.

When we left Kingaru at dawn on the sixth of April, not just I but at least half the porters and soldiers were enfeebled and far from recovered. Nevertheless, we were all happy to leave the place that had brought us so close to the abyss.

Asmani, who had taken down my tent, fetched my donkey and helped me into the saddle. In the distance I glimpsed Stanley through the morning mist, getting ready to mount his donkey. But no: to my surprise he gave the still-weak Selim a boost and then began striding out of Kingaru next to our guide, Hamadi, who was playfully waving the American flag.

So Stanley didn't give me even the small satisfaction of seeing him bounce along on donkeyback. If he couldn't ride a horse, he walked. An admiring murmur arose among the porters, and Stanley responded by turning and raising his fist with a smile. Somehow, he was always capable of turning a defeat into a victory.

Not a single inhabitant of the village came out to witness our departure. Only a small scabby dog barked at us.

In my memory, the days that followed blur into one another in a feverish fog. I have no idea of the chronology of events, I can't remember having performed any tasks, and I had only the occasional word with Stanley. All my energy went into trying to sit, lie, or hang on to the damn donkey.

Thus I have only a few fleeting but extremely clear images of the eleven-day journey from Kingaru to Simbamwenni. The porters were still weakened by illness and often totally exhausted. One day, when the sun was at its zenith, we stopped to rest in a verdant grove by a creek. The porters dragged themselves to the water and simply fell into it. Some just lay there among the rocks in the clear-flowing current, gazing up at the treetops with empty eyes. Others wept and wailed like little children. When we started out again, two of them stayed by the creek, and I felt their stares like flames on my back as I left that spot, as always bringing up the rear of the caravan.

I still resented my position. I forced Saburi to walk behind me, but that just made matters worse. I started imagining that he would stab me in the back at any moment. Sometimes I had such a vivid sensation of that knife point at my back that I reached out behind me.

There was always something looming back there: a great forest bird swooping down into a ravine and being swallowed up by the greenery; dark clouds and rumbling thunder on the horizon; monkeys staring from treetops; a snake slithering between the hind legs of a panic-stricken donkey; a rock rolling off a precipice only a couple of yards behind me; all kinds of strange noises.

One evening Hamadi offered me some palm wine. I got good and drunk and staggered into Stanley's tent, where I made a big fuss and knocked things over. At first Stanley laughed at me, but he soon became impatient and evicted me with a kick in the pants. Asmani carried me back to my tent. The next morning I thought I'd die.

One of our porters ran away; surprising, really, that not more of them have done likewise. He was captured and given collective punishment. Stanley made us stand in a long line: first me, then stone-faced Bombay and one-handed Mabruki, who worships Stanley, then all the soldiers and porters. Thus I had the honor of giving the culprit his first lash of the donkey whip. After every member of the expedition had struck him with the whip, his back was quite torn up, the flesh hanging down in tatters. The blood attracted swarms of flies that disappeared only after someone had covered his wounds with a sticky paste. His screams, before he was given this soothing medication, sounded as if they came from beyond the sun-baked plain. They sounded as if they came from all directions at once.

One day when the sun was at its highest and hottest point in the sky, we passed a slave caravan climbing a steep slope. Below, behind them, the savannah shimmered like a lake. The slaves were naked, shackled together. They shone with sweat, and around their ankles where the chain was attached you could see red and yellow patches of blood and pus. They were carrying enormous loads, and their demeanor was desperate. While a few of them hung their heads, the majority seemed excited to the point of madness. Their breathing was rapid, their eyes stared, they uttered shrill cries and laughed hysterically. The slave trader, a slender Arab with piercing eyes, kept his restless cargo together by means of soldiers who marched back and forth with their whips, maintaining order. The rear was brought up by the Arab's harem, a bizarre group of women and children swathed in light fluttering robes. The youngest children sat in rows on donkeys, a little idyll attached to the tail of hell.

After we had passed the noisy slave caravan, the stillness of the surrounding countryside seemed more intense. My donkey and the porters ahead of us moved along without a sound. No one sang, no one spoke. Silence reigned. Only the sun's fire sounded like a very faint, faraway rumbling.

The sunsets are like cool springwater in a parched throat. The lengthening shadows, the burning horizon, the silhouettes of the acacias, and the blue mountains all seem immersed in prayer. Donkeys and goats stand stock-still, as if quietly weeping, though a few bound about as if intoxicated by the very air. Even I become reconciled with existence. A call sounds as if from the far side of a lake. People move in a sanctuary.

My accordion, which I don't trust the porters to carry, always sits in front of me on the donkey's neck. No matter how I position it, the donkey's movements cause it to sound rhythmically, forcing a high note and a low one out in a sort of wheeze. It is not a loud noise, I'm the only one who can hear it, but it bothers me. It sounds like a death rattle.

A couple of times we caught up with our fourth caravan. Due to illness—or indolence, according to Stanley—it hasn't been able to keep up a satisfactory marching pace. But we have not seen anything of brother Farquhar. That too disturbs Stanley. He is afraid that Farquhar has pulled ahead and started up his own expedition. I miss him. I have no one to talk to—except, of course, Saburi.

Only a few days before we arrived in Simbamwenni, we met yet another caravan, this one carrying three hundred ivory tusks. Like the slave caravan, it was on its way to the coast and Zanzibar. The Arab nobleman who owned all that ivory invited Stanley and me to a meal. The lavish table looked as if he received daily supplies from Zanzibar, Baghdad, and Paris. Nothing was lacking. With dainty gestures he offered us white rice, spicy chicken, some sort of pancakes, fresh bread, sauces with bits of beef in them, and, to crown it all, a mound of tasty fruit. As I had begun to recover from my Kingaru illness, I was able to enjoy the food.

The Arab was coming from Ujiji, and that aroused Stanley's interest. He assailed our host with a multitude of questions. Whom had he met? What were things like in Ujiji?

"There is a large Arab colony in Ujiji; we trade from there via Unyanyembe to Zanzibar. There is unrest between Ujiji and Unyanyembe. A terrible chieftain, Mirambo, is constantly attacking our caravans. There will be a war soon, between his soldiers and our men. We must be able to travel safely between Ujiji and Zanzibar. It is a condition of our existence."

Mirambo. There was something about the name that impressed me. The Arab's way of pronouncing it commanded respect.

Toward the end of the meal the Arab told us, as if to entertain us, about a strange white man who was staying in Ujiji. The blacks thought of him as an eccentric Arab.

"He is an odd fellow, but really a good man who has stayed in Africa a little too long. He may not live much longer: when I left Ujiji, he was very ill, and my people had to help him with the simplest things."

"What is the name of this man?" Stanley asked.

"I do not know his name."

"It must be him. D'you hear, Shaw? Livingstone is alive!"

"Who is Livingstone?" I asked.

Stanley stared at me as if I should know the name. Then he got to his feet and began to laugh. He doesn't laugh often. It is an awful sound.

"Listen, Shaw, don't ever forget that name—Livingstone! He is one of the most important men in the world."

Now it was the Arab's turn to laugh.

"Oh, so you regard him as an important man. Interesting. Could it be he is a kinsman? Or are you perhaps confusing him with someone else?"

"Unfortunately, we are not related, but it must be him. Tell me, does he have many followers?"

"That I do not know. I really do not know what he does. He has no head for business. Sometimes he is busy drawing strange maps; he claims he is mapping the area. He told a good friend of mine who brings him food that he had discovered the source of the Nile in the wilderness on the far side of Lake Tanganyika. No, I do not think this is the man you have in mind. This is just a peculiar old man."

"But he is one of the world's great explorers!"

The Arab became serious when he saw how excited his guest was.

"Perhaps we who have done business here for a few generations see matters a little differently. But I beg you, help yourselves to the food. In a little while I will call the slave girls."

The Arab grew more and more amiable and jovial,

while Stanley's mood was one of distaste and impatience. Our host lounged on deep cushions and made conversation about food, business, and women, casting friendly glances upon us from black eyes half concealed by heavy lids.

Stanley thanked him perfunctorily and left. I stayed a while, enjoying the delicacies of the table. It is a pity Arabs don't use alcohol.

On the way back to my tent I was joined by one of the Arab's female slaves, a none too young woman who showed no respect for me. When I lit the lamp in my tent, she burst out laughing at the sight of my clothes and then started examining everything I owned. For a Negress, she was uncommonly light-skinned. Perhaps she was part Arab. Although we did not have a single word in common, she managed to beg in the most explicit manner. She kept on begging even in the very act of love and did not have sense enough to lie still but wriggled hither and thither in her eagerness to inspect the contents of my "home." I was insulted and wished I hadn't let her inside.

But these are only a few isolated moments seen in a cold bright light amidst an otherwise opaque and grainy fog. I don't know what is happening to me. Am I beginning to lose my memory? Or is it all just a temporary change caused by the fever I had in Kingaru?

The porters and soldiers no longer harass me. Except for Saburi and maybe Asmani, they pay me no attention. Hamadi banters with me, as he does with everybody. Often I wonder what my actual role is in this expedition, as I don't fulfill any visible function. Well, it may be revealed in due course.

Even Stanley ignores me unless he needs someone upon whom to vent his frustrations. Although we often dine together, we hardly talk. But there was a real eruption on our first evening here in Simbamwenni.

To give the background: As we approached the Lion City on the other side of the river, the grit and slag of recent days seemed to wash out of my mind. Once again, the march was something that concerned me, and I felt my strength return. With Bombay and Hamadi I planned our fording of the river. Stanley was taken across quickly to pay his respects to the Sultana. He left the responsibility for the crossing of the pack train to me, not to Bombay, as I had expected. With quick resolve, Bombay and I managed to lead the terrified donkeys across a turbulent river that came up to their shoulders. In just half an hour we had brought across both animals and people, without a single mishap. We didn't lose one load, and there were no injuries of any kind.

That same evening, at dusk, I was sitting in front of my newly pitched tent when Selim came shuffling over to tell me that Stanley wanted to see me.

"He's angry."

He was more than angry, he was absolutely furious. His body was rigid, as if in convulsion, and his dry face was an awful purple. With an outstretched finger he pointed at a bale of cloth lying in the middle of his tent.

"Touch it!"

I touched it. The lower half of the bale was a little damp, but otherwise it seemed to be intact.

"What's the matter?"

"The matter? Why, you goddamn pirate! You're so

73

used to water you can't even tell that this material is waterlogged—ruined!"

"It will dry out. I can't stop the rain."

"No, but you can drive the donkeys across the river so that my cloth gets soaked. Dry out! You will dry every last bit of that cloth with your own hands, or I'll make you pay for it!"

I became quite cold and clear-headed. For the first time, I felt I had the upper hand. Stanley was raging on about a trifle. To top it all, my work that afternoon had been exemplary. Even Bombay had looked at me in surprise when I displayed such decisiveness.

Calmly, sure that he would realize his mistake and rectify it, I stated my case and said:

"I demand an apology. Otherwise I will leave the expedition and return to Bagamoyo first thing in the morning."

Stanley turned on his heel and vanished outside. I remained in the tent, waiting for him to calm down, come back, and restore things to normal.

He reappeared at the entrance to the tent a few minutes later. He was beaming.

"I accept your resignation. I shall retain your gear and your possessions as recompense for the advance I paid you in Zanzibar. Mabruki is already striking your tent, and he will bring your belongings to me. You will leave camp tonight. Goodbye."

The very skin on my body seemed to lose all its moisture; I shriveled completely within seconds.

Stanley ordered his guard to escort me out of the tent. As I staggered into the darkening night with a rifle muzzle at my back, I found myself trapped under a milky glass bell that enclosed me in a stifling gaseous world. Only when we passed my tent, which Mabruki was folding up assisted by two soldiers, did a primitive instinct for self-preservation wake in me. I ran back to Stanley's tent, the guard yelling and chasing after me. I was sure he couldn't bring himself to shoot a white man in the back.

My return didn't surprise Stanley. He smiled indulgently.

"So you realize how poorly you reacted?"

I nodded.

"Apologize."

"I'm sorry."

"On your knees."

I did that too.

He came over and helped me back to my feet. One hand caressed my neck.

"And now we'll just forget about it. I don't bear grudges. We may disagree, but as sensible white men we know how to resolve conflicts and be friends again. Do we not?"

He produced a bottle of gin and two glasses. Selim was ordered to have my tent pitched again. We toasted and drank. Stanley was in a wonderful mood. He invited me to sit down and regaled me with stories of his earlier voyages—to the Wild West, to Asia—until the hour approached midnight. By that time the bottle was gone, and I had imbibed the lion's share.

Nevertheless, as I walked back to my tent, I didn't feel the least bit intoxicated. But I did feel as if I were floating five inches above the ground, swimming through air that was a black, oily liquid.

I was not unhappy. I was pleased that Stanley was in a good mood again and that we had had a nice time. It didn't happen all that often. Our falling-out was a trifle after all, as he himself had said.

There's a full moon tonight. What do I really care about Stanley or the whole bizarre expedition? It is an important evening. I sit in front of my tent writing by moonlight, without a lantern. The day's rain has ceased, the sky is full of stars. Like the men in camp, nature's awesome power has laid itself to rest by the fires of the night and given itself over to an unhurried world with no particular goal. I hear talk and laughter. Someone is playing rhythms on an *mbira,* and drums are beating within Simbamwenni's fortifications.

This peace lies close to the final zero, annihilation. Never before have I felt so near to death. My thoughts are lit from within, my brain is made of the clearest rock crystal. Time does not stand still. It simply is. I find myself on the point of an arrow that is on its way back to the bow, not forward to a target. I am a child about to slide into the moist warm womb of its mother, and I become pregnant with myself. Permanently pregnant, just like the female figurine Saburi gave me. I have come full circle, and my thought moves straight into the slow, fading tick of a clock.

Stanley is moving forward, in the opposite direction. He too has changed; perhaps he has lost his mind. He is more brutal than ever before, but also more senti-mental. In his delirium he calls out for Father Livingstone, the old eccentric in Ujiji, the one the Arab told us about. Stanley swings the whip with one hand, and dries his tears with the other.

Tonight I put off from shore. The river is flowing slowly, and the beach is crowded with elephants moving in the dust in a shared rhythm. In the water the curved backs of hippopotamuses rise and sink, and crocodiles slide soundlessly into the black current. They are all kin to the whales, whose cries reverberate in the bodies of the great beasts of the land. There is no tenderness comparable to the tenderness you can feel for the bodies of the great animals. For the wild.

Saburi often speaks to me of the dead. Tonight, I understand him: the dead have laid their hands on my shoulder. I am at the turning point.

I am emptied out. I have never seen more clearly, understood more deeply. There is nothing to understand. All you have to do is let the sun burn through your body, the water flow over your limbs, the wind fill your chest.

Asmani, that huge laughing personification of kindness, has just paid me a visit. He offered me a bowl of palm wine. I drank and returned the bowl. We did not say a word.

The wild. It isn't dark, it isn't light. It is a great memory. And I exist right next to it.

Stanley is ill.

Makata, Kiora, Mpwapwa

Now my days are a blur—a heavy rock tumbling down a ravine, a labored breath in a room emptied of air.

Even though my body still has the same external volume as before, my weight has dropped considerably. I have become porous. There are times when my feet lose touch with the ground and I float an inch or so above it. Yet I feel ever more weary.

Right now I'm sharing a small hut with cockroaches and white ants, God knows where. These white ants have a soul. They make collective decisions, and nothing can keep them from carrying out those decisions. They choose the victims of their hunger and their destructive urges with great care. Stanley's hut is teeming with them; there are none in Saburi's or Asmani's.

Stanley is an Other. His body is not part of the caravan's body. And it is only he who is an Other: even his most devoted lackeys belong to the greater body. But he does not. The white ants know that.

* * *

I don't recall on what date we left Simbamwenni. It had rained a great deal the preceding twenty-four hours, and it was hard to get started in the trampled mud of the camp. Once again we crossed the river, which now carried much more water. For the first time I noticed that there were many women and children in our caravan. Weeping and shrill cries echoed over the water as they crossed on a makeshift hanging bridge we had rigged up.

It took us a week to reach the Makata swamp. Stanley insisted on forcing us down into it; against all advice he chose to lead us through that hell. Bombay didn't say anything. At the time, he had been stripped of his captaincy, and his silence rang in our ears.

A strange man joined us at Simbamwenni. Stanley didn't hire him; he isn't paid any wages. He is a deaf mute and probably insane. No one has heard him say a word. He is as tall as Asmani, much leaner, but just as strong. On his thick, wide lips lingers a perennial smile that is neither happy nor sad. He keeps his face averted, his eyes gaze inward. The only things he does well are walking and carrying. The porters take advantage of this by turns and saddle him with enormous loads. They feed him but otherwise pretend he doesn't exist. When they give him food or lift a load on top of his head, they treat him with seriousness and respect. Every morning, when he has been given a new load, a flash of happiness, a gleam of satisfaction, seems to light up his face. When we rest or make camp, he finds it hard to stop. He keeps walking around in wide, restless circles. Only when the load has been raised to his head and the caravan starts moving does his stride become easy and powerful again.

Saburi claims that as long as "the Bearer," as he is called, is with us, no disaster can befall our caravan.

Since Simbamwenni, Saburi takes his meals alone. Asmani is the only one who talks to him. The others fear and shun him.

Stanley's dog: I had become fond of it. Now it is dead. It had followed its master across Europe, America, and Asia, and it was the only animal I've ever seen that knew how to laugh. It did not jump up and down to express joy and recognition, as other dogs do. It was given to malicious glee and savored absurdities. When it first saw the Bearer stalking around in circles while everybody else was lying down resting, it turned away and laughed. You could tell it was laughing just by looking at the muscles in its back and belly; from its muzzle came a sound somewhere between coughing and panting. The dog stayed clear of Stanley, always maintaining a distance of a couple of yards. It never had to obey him because it knew how to slink off just as Stanley was looking for it. It did not enjoy hunting, and once, when Stanley put it on a rope leash and took it into the jungle, it showed up in camp again in a matter of minutes, looking bored.

It begged for food by pretending to limp or by crawling obsequiously on its belly. Every time you gave it something you felt it had pulled a fast one on you.

The dog had only one friend, a donkey. When we rested, they used to lie next to each other in the shade. But it did run around with the village dogs and mated with some of them, even though it was twice as large.

As long as it was alive, I had the feeling that everything was still normal. But it died in the Makata swamp.

The Makata valley is an unpopulated savannah with many game animals. It is not a dry high plain but a boggy low-lying flatland with dense bamboo thickets growing around slow-running watercourses. No people anywhere. Here and there, the odd palm or other large tree with exposed roots rises above grass and shrubbery. The stifling miasma makes one feverish and heavy in the head.

One early morning—we were camped by the edge of the swamp—Stanley called me to his tent, which surprised me because we had just finished a simple, quiet breakfast together. It was time for a flogging again. Selim had told on Stanley's cook, who had been eating scraps from Stanley's table.

I took the cook to a spot behind Stanley's tent.

"Scream!" I whispered to him, lightly slapping his clothed back.

He shook his head and looked at me with scorn. He had had enough. I could tell from his eyes that he was ready to leave us.

Stanley helped him along, using the same method he'd used on me: dismissal and expulsion from camp. But he vanished immediately, and Stanley lost both a repentant sinner and a good cook. For a long time Stanley stood staring at the bamboo grove that had swallowed the man up. He couldn't understand. Where was the mistake? In his head or in the cook's? His head gave no answer.

* * *

The trees around the Makata swamp were shimmering in the heat. Steam was rising from the ground, bubbling out of the muddy water. Nothing else made a sound; the birdsong and the croaking of the frogs didn't commence until early evening. The swamp was a feverishly hot lung. The closer we came to its center, the more implacably Stanley made one wrong decision after another. A mere trifle kept us in this insalubrious region for several days.

The day before we arrived at Makata we had traversed a wide plain of reddish soil. Stanley was proceeding at a breakneck pace, and the cart, pulled by Bombay and some soldiers, fell behind. Selim, in whose charge the cart had originally been, was now permitted to walk without a load or weapons. Bombay, the soldiers, and the cart arrived in camp late at night. Stanley was furious with them. Bombay and his soldiers were gray in the face with fatigue and dust. In a voice that sounded like jagged ice, Bombay told Stanley that part of the load had been stolen while they were pulling the cart out of a waterhole. Stanley was apoplectic and finally shouted, beside himself with rage:

"You are no longer a captain! You are demoted! And tomorrow you will go back and fetch that stolen property!"

Bombay did not reply, he just walked away. He had a wicked-sounding cough.

And so we waited on the edge of that infernal swamp for several days while Bombay went on his fool's errand to retrieve the stolen goods. Three other soldiers were given the even more foolish assignment of finding the renegade cook; if necessary, they were to pursue him all the way back to Simbamwenni.

In the course of those days, half of us fell ill. Perhaps Stanley wanted us sick—perhaps he wanted us to be in poor shape for the attack against Makata's heart.

Although he suffered from his enforced idleness, the Bearer remained healthy, tramping back and forth in the mud. In a way, his was the greatest loss: he was deprived of the only thing in life he valued—bearing burdens.

It took only two days for me to come down with a fever. When Stanley noticed my condition, he ordered me to go after the men who were looking for the cook. Was this cat-and-mouse game going to destroy us all? Before I left, Saburi whispered to me:

"The great master carries evil inside him. He cannot help it, he does not want to do evil, but he is forced to do it. If he were a black man, we would kill him. Now he may kill us all here at Makata."

I'm often envious of Stanley. He delights in the setbacks of others and relishes his own successes. He sleeps well. Even in dreams he is master of the rules of the game. The rest of us carry the taste of death in our mouths. He rinses his every morning with good European mouthwash.

We are animals. He is not. We are the vibrating air right above the god of the fire. He is the one who pours water on the fire.

"Do you think Stanley believes in God?" I asked Saburi.

"He stands outside of God," Saburi replied, and picked up the female figurine he had given me. He was sitting in my tent. He began to breathe deeply through his nose, in short, intense spurts. His flat nostrils beat faster and faster, then slowed, and slowed some more. I laughed.

"You're just a snuffling Negro, Saburi, don't think you're anything special. And I'm just a ridiculous white man who has to laugh."

After a while, he stopped breathing altogether, and I began to feel that I was suffocating. When he started breathing again, after several minutes, he said:

"At night, the white ants crawl into his head. They jump in through his ears, mouth, nose, eyes, and come out again through the openings down below. And yet he lives."

Then he went on talking in his own language, which I don't understand. His body shook as if in a fever, the whites of his eyes flashed, the blood was pounding in his temples. Finally he collapsed in a heap on the ground. He looked dead.

The porters and soldiers came and watched. They said nothing and kept a respectful distance. Half an hour later Saburi got up and walked away.

Saburi: fool, prophet, animal? He is both ridiculous and demonic.

Right now I have a craving for alcohol. British gin, preferably.

Something is happening to my handwriting. It looks different, uneven, but pretty in a childish way.

* * *

Outside my tent a few young men and women are sitting and talking things over. One of them is jolly Hamadi, who recently bought himself a slave. He apparently has several at home. It pleases me to hear them. They are sharing words with one another.

Now a girl in her teens brings them food. They all stop talking. Her body is straight and soft, both. (Why are European women often so rigid and bent?) When she sits on her haunches, soft folds appear around her waist and hips. Her firm breasts sway as she arranges the pot of food. She rubs her nose with the back of her hand. The others draw closer to the pot, as if they want to be as near the ground as possible before they start eating. One of them sticks a long little finger in his ear and twists it around, another sucks her lips in and makes a smacking sound, a third scratches his scalp. Then they eat, slowly. Negroes always eat slowly, especially when they're starving.

They stick the tips of their fingers into the pot and smear the food onto their lower lips. Noisily they lick and suck fingers shiny with palm oil. Then, with a relaxed motion, they extend the right arm back to the pot—now someone may make a remark—and help themselves again. When the pot is empty and they have sucked their fingers clean, they get up, not all at once but casually, at random, and drink some water from a bowl that's been placed nearby. They take a few deep draughts, then rinse their mouths and spit the water out in a quick jet. Drinking and rinsing are done with their backs turned to their comrades. Then they resume their lifelong exchange of words.

85

It is their way of conversing and eating that makes me feel hungry, excited, thirsty, and eager to talk. It can't be their food, which I've never even tasted, nor can it be their stories, since I don't know their language; it's the sounds and gestures that get to me. But I haven't been invited to share a meal, not once. They believe I am an alien, and thus I become one.

After half a day's march I ran into the soldiers who had been sent to look for the cook. They had gone all the way to Simbamwenni and encountered difficulties with the Sultana. By virtue of luck, cunning, and the assistance of an Arab, they were still alive, but they hadn't seen a trace of the cook.

We turned around. In the afternoon, the fever sapped my strength: I lay on the donkey's back, and the soldiers walked on either side of it in order to catch me if I fell off. I remember a white light, an ugly, monotonous plain, grass like knife blades, soil as hard as rock. It was a landscape that consumed my will to live. The soldiers' sweaty bodies gave off a rank smell, and the donkey's bristly neck chafed my face. I remember how my cheek and mouth slid over the soldiers' bare shoulders when they boosted me up again after a fall.

Just before we entered camp I noticed that Bombay was walking along with us.

I was carried to my tent. I heard Stanley, outside, encouraging the soldiers to heap scorn on their former captain. I could tell from their voices that they were merely obeying orders; they sounded frightened.

Bombay entered my tent, gave me a baleful stare, and put a ripe mango fruit on the ground beside me.

Without a word, he left me again. I was pleased to be in his thoughts.

Around the Makata swamp the presence of the great animal bodies is palpable. Here and there we caught glimpses of game in the thickets. They always turned one side toward us. Only once a gigantic elephant stepped forward, ears extended, trunk raised. For a few seconds he was a single massive concentration of attention. Then he decided we were too insignificant and moved on.

The tent canvas was sweating fever. Once again I found myself in an animal body, kneaded by its digestive organs, waiting to be squeezed through intestines and anus, to end up as a pile of steaming dung by a lone baobab tree.

My decay has begun.

Practically all of us became ill at Makata. Asmani was the first to complain of fever, headaches, and pains in the small of his back. A couple of days later, just before Stanley began the march to the heart of Makata, red pustules appeared on Asmani's forehead, nose, and upper lip. In a few days his superb body changed into a pitiful caricature of its former beauty. He reminded me of the skeletons of water buffalo, rhinoceroses, and elephants we had seen on our journey. His eyes glared out of dark cavities, bespeaking a panic as silent as death, a crystal-clear insight. The red spots were death's little labels. His mouth was frozen in an embarrassed grin.

Saburi tended this gigantic skeletal child, who cried out shrilly at night, like a hyena. Stanley threatened to shoot him if he didn't keep quiet.

On a morning that seemed like one great sigh, we started out toward the heart of Makata. Asmani staggered along, chin trembling, eyes running. Saburi stayed next to him. The others gave them a wide berth. I hung on to my donkey and watched them trail after the caravan.

After a few miles, when the water almost came up to the donkey's belly, I fell off and nearly drowned. I shouted myself hoarse, but no one came. It was completely still, like the silence that follows a rifleshot on the high seas. After an eternity in which time canceled itself and the sun stood still in the sky and the leeches launched their attack, two porters came to the rescue. They helped me back into the saddle and vanished again. The donkey's flanks streamed with water mixed with my sweat. I hung on tight to saddle and reins. If I had to die, the donkey would perish with me.

The swamp was an inland sea. After another eternity, forgotten by men and alone with a scornful god, I came across a single man lying half immersed in the water. He propped his back and arms against some tree roots, yelled, and pointed at the donkey. His face was covered with red pustules. As I passed him, he threw himself at me and grabbed my leg with incredible strength. I kicked, cried, cursed, and shouted before he let go. Then I had to laugh out loud. The donkey staggered on, driven by my convulsive laughter.

I saw Stanley's dog on a dry tussock. It was lying on its side, but it raised its head a little and gave me a mild and mournful look. On the last stretch through the swamp, Saburi caught up with me. His weeping and lamentation consoled me. It was still difficult to stop laughing.

Before we reached dry land again, we came across four porters and two soldiers: twelve eyes stared at me, twelve hands reached out for me, sixty frantic fingers tried to grab my legs. What frightened me most was that none of them had those red spots.

All this took place in broad, dazzling daylight, in air so humid that it had to be forced into one's lungs. I did not catch a single glimpse of Stanley. But he may stand outside of God, and I saw God all day.

And yet what I remember most clearly is a waterbuck that turned tail and vanished in great effortless bounds.

The days are white light and sweat running off my eyebrows. Everything is clear, too clear. Dazzling.

The moonlit nights are one long bout of insomnia. Oil everywhere, blue, slow-flowing oil. Something is going on in the pale night, something that cannot rest. When I move around in camp, everything is in motion; when I stand still, everything comes to a halt. The shadows are always prepared.

On these moonlit nights I breathe through my mouth. The mild light is suspended between inner ear and throat. My head is open.

The predators are roaring themselves out of their bodies. The crickets are beside themselves.

On the other side of Makata—paradise. Hell and paradise, always neighboring countries. A highland with sparkling water, lush vegetation, a village with healthy people and abundant food. All around one could see the broad backsides of women stooping down to till the soil.

When I had pitched my tent with the help of a porter, I lay down to sleep. I awoke to a great silence. It was so quiet that I realized that the open space in front of my tent must be crowded with people. I crawled out.

In the middle of paradise stood Saburi, mute, devastated, sullen. Around him stood silent, resolute soldiers and porters. No way out for Saburi now. He had been found guilty of the deaths of Asmani and the others.

I understood. This was the echo from heaven. After Makata, something had to change. It was all so simple and clear. Saburi had to atone.

Stanley and Selim were the only ones not present; they might as well have been in Europe.

To fall into an abyss, narrow and deep.

I remembered the damp cobblestones of London, the fog under the bridges, my breath steaming one early morning. My mother's dress that smelled of cabbage.

Bombay asked Saburi if he was guilty. He nodded. Some tried to strike him, spit at him, but Bombay fended them off. He picked up his rifle and took Saburi away. A distant report. Bombay returned, his face an ebony carving.

I was present, I was one of them. And yet I was separated from them, as if made of another material. I was not able to grieve as the others were.

* * *

I have sneaked an illicit look at Stanley's notes. In them, he says simply that the dog and a few porters died in the Makata swamp. What does Stanley know that he didn't know in Zanzibar? He is so far away.

Is there anything I haven't lost? If so, what would it be? Can madness be anything but strength? Am I mad or strong?

At night I hear children crying. I don't know if the noise comes from the steadily expanding families of the porters or from within my own head. But I don't like it. It arouses a kind of tenderness.

It only takes a few days for a camp to produce an oppressive stench: rotting food scraps, excrement in shallow latrine holes, animal droppings, the sour smell of human and animal bodies. In the heat it all blends into a nauseating smog that washes over you in waves. I've often seen village dogs eating each other's shit before it even hit the ground.

When I hear Stanley's shrill voice, my teeth hurt.

Why does one travel, move across the surface of the earth to places one has not seen before? When I see a plain, a forest, a mountain, or a waterway for the first time, I often sense a kind of cold piety emerging within me. No memories to cloud the eye. A frosty reverence. Is that what one is looking for?

It is surprising how well one can get by without alcohol.

* * *

On the silent plain the porters make a lot of noise. In the noisy forest they're silent.

On the plain you can hear the grass moving. The acacias, clipper ships of the savannah, sail soundlessly in the vibrating hot air that pours across the plain. Sometimes there is the thunder of thousands of hooves.

In the forest monkeys chatter, birds twitter and scream, small animals rustle, and big beasts crash away in flight. The forest is a cool edifice, a humid lung that smells of acid and decay. The sun flickers through the tree canopy, creates columns of dazzling light. The eye has trouble adjusting to the contrast between light and dark. The gigantic tree trunks, overgrown with mosses and wound about with lianas, look invincible. And so the most powerful sound in the jungle is the crash of an ancient tree when it falls.

Fevers, elephantiasis, gastric fever, leprosy, smallpox, trachoma, syphilis, dysentery. Stanley takes copious notes. He knows the names of many more diseases.

My mirror broke in Kingaru. Then, it didn't bother me much, but after the Makata swamp it's a catastrophe.

Stanley does not permit me to look into his mirror. Every time I'm called to his tent or hut, he stands there scrutinizing himself. He knows my longing. Meticulously he examines the skin around his nose, makes faces, turns his head this way and that to see himself from different angles. He opens his mouth wide, stands on tiptoe, and stares down into his throat.

I doubt that he really sees anything.

* * *

As we were approaching Kiora we heard rumors that Farquhar's troop was already there. This pleased me as much as Stanley's illness in Simbamwenni. Before we even reached the village, we could tell by the stench that Farquhar's caravan had been there for many days. His camp lay in a gloomy dell on the outskirts of the village. The tents were poorly pitched, and no one came to greet us. There wasn't a single donkey in sight. A couple of soldiers were lazing around a fire. They looked at us without interest when we made our noisy entry into the village.

I would be able to talk to a human being, pass time with a comrade, share a meal with someone who respected me. Farquhar: wise, calm, and generous.

Stanley had to produce his whip and shout and carry on before the soldiers got to their feet. After a short period of confusion, they went into a tent and came out carrying a gigantic shape resembling a man. At first I thought it was some albino monster, then that it was a local deity stuffed to the size of four men and swathed in dirty lengths of fabric. Finally I imagined it to be a freak of nature the likes of which European science had not yet seen. It was a tremendously engorged human figure.

It was Farquhar.

Stanley stopped shouting and walked up to examine him the way one would examine a rotting cadaver. Then he strode off briskly, without a word.

I went to Farquhar and took his hand. It was a bloated excrescence. Tears ran down his shiny, swollen cheeks. I asked him if he was ill, if he was in pain. He just shook his head. When the porters lifted him up to carry him back into the tent, he said in a voice that bubbled forth out of all that fat:

"I am swelling to death."

A few hours later he was carried to Stanley's tent. There I watched him receive a full dressing-down for drunkenness and whoring, for mistreating the donkeys and so causing their deaths, for slowing down the third caravan's progress, and for paying too much tribute to the chiefs. Farquhar wheezed back that he had done his best.

After a while Stanley's mood improved, and he began to examine Farquhar. Before squeezing the man's swollen legs, he put on a pair of gloves he'd been keeping in a medicine cabinet. The stink of Farquhar's body did not faze him: he even pulled off the loosely draped pieces of cloth and laid bare a colossal penis hanging heavily between fat thighs. Farquhar let Stanley squeeze it, milk it, and take measurements of both length and circumference. All this was duly recorded. Stanley read his notes out loud: Bright's disease, hypertrophy, elephantiasis.

When the examination was over, Stanley sat down in a chair and chuckled.

"If by some miracle you manage to get back to Europe, you can get a job in a freak show. People will flock to see you by the thousands. Your penis could make you famous."

Farquhar's expression did not change. It was like the expression on the face of a watchful boar.

I spent several days sitting in Farquhar's tent. He lay on his cot, breathing heavily, and drank vast quantities of water. I told him what had happened to me. He did not comment. I don't think he even listened.

One day he surprised me by asking:

"Do you know why he took the two of us along? So that we should die and he survive. You must kill him!"

We marched on. Six men carried Farquhar. In the villages we passed through the people prostrated themselves when they saw him. Children and chickens scattered in all directions. Dogs growled.

I was put in charge of that goddamned cart, which always caused problems. One afternoon, I and the porters who were pulling it fell seriously behind the rest of the caravan. Stanley would not stop to wait for us when we got stuck in the mud or had difficulty on steep ascents.

Night fell before we managed to catch up. We had to lie down on the ground right where we were and try to sleep. When we rejoined the caravan the following day, Stanley gave me orders to flog the porters in whose company I had spent the night.

Farquhar, who had been quiet at first, began to scream uncontrollably during the days of our approach to Mpwapwa. He gave a stream of orders for floggings and executions, right and left. At first, he threw everyone into a panic, until they realized that Stanley just laughed at him. The relief was great, and they all started making fun of Farquhar. Even the scrawniest little porter laughed and spat in his face when Stanley wasn't around.

Slowly we proceeded across a barren steppe. The silence and the dry wind carried a sense of cold menace. In the end I came to welcome Farquhar's screaming. Decapitation, flogging, castration. His curses sustained us.

For one whole day the porters and soldiers imitated Farquhar. They puffed up their cheeks and shouted atrocities at each another. The marching pace picked up, and through all these merry expletives—even I joined in when I grew too weary—you could now and again hear Farquhar's own cracked voice.

The memories stick to my palate like overly sweet candies. I don't know what to do with them. Inexorably they point to my present condition.

Autumn in an English garden. Someone riding calmly by. A bite of apple. The night's frost still clinging to the surface of the ground. Boiled cabbage and Mother's armpits.

Farquhar's elephant feet that have begun to rot. His childish weeping, his unbridled appetite.

British gin.

I don't know another person as true to himself as Stanley. He lives every hour of his life according to his convictions. How does he manage? Or is it a disease?

On one occasion Farquhar responded to me with absolute fury: when I asked if I could borrow his mirror. He yelled that he had smashed it a long time ago. I'll never forgive him that.

It took over a week before I began to miss Saburi and Asmani. First I vomited, and then I wept, bent over my trunk holding the female figurine.

There, inside my trunk, I saw Asmani's gigantic carcass, his death's-head covered with thin skin, that horrifying smile on his lips. Saburi's mute nod to Bombay's
question, how he had shrunk and turned blacker and
blacker.

Bombay appeared at the tent flap. I threw the figurine at him.

"Murderer!"

It struck him in the forehead and dark red blood ran
down his black nose. For a moment I thought he was
going to kill me. But he just placed the figurine carefully by my side.

"You need it. Next time you attack me, I kill you."

Bombay will outlive all of us. He alone will stand by
Stanley's deathbed.

Farquhar is a rotting whale.

Stanley invited me and Farquhar to dinner. He wanted
us to celebrate the success of our expedition up to this
point. We proposed toasts with British gin. He made a
speech in which he maintained that everything had
gone far better than expected, despite the carelessness
and indolence of certain people. The weakest links had
perished, just as he had anticipated. The stronger the
weakest link, the stronger the entire body, he said.

"The eyes of the whole world are upon us! We have
great cause to be happy."

Farquhar and I sat and listened to his hour-long
oration in silence. After the success of our expedition,
European settlers would come streaming into Africa.
The savannah would be plowed and sown with wheat
and rye. The wild beasts would be shot or domesti-

cated, railroads would be built across the continent, people would ride around on fleet-footed zebras, and the forests would be cut down for buildings and fuel for the factories that would spring up by the railroads. The Negroes would be baptized and taught to work. On the navigable rivers, shining white British steamers would transport goods and people.

"Even if the two of you should die on this expedition, you have reason to be proud! Your defective bodies and vacillating minds have participated in a great enterprise. Perhaps I shall soon reveal to you the central task of our expedition: to find the light that shall guide the hand of the future."

Farquhar didn't seem to be listening. He just kept shoveling food into his mouth. After a while, I too stopped paying attention; Stanley's ceaseless flow of words made me ravenous as well. I stuffed myself with delicacies until I felt sick. The temperature in the tent seemed to rise under his bombast, and I was close to the limit of my endurance.

I rose hastily and said that the whole goddamned expedition—and its leader in particular—was like the rectum of a dysentery victim. And I said it was my dearest wish to see Stanley roast in hell, for time and eternity.

My words made Farquhar smile. He looked terrible. Stanley came at me and knocked me down with a powerful punch. It was amazing. How could that frail body pack such a wallop?

Lying there on the floor, I started laughing. Stanley kicked me, but I couldn't help myself.

"Stop! I'm going home!" I shouted.

Stanley called Bombay and instructed him to strike my tent and take me and my personal belongings to the outskirts of the camp. He also told Farquhar that he intended to leave him in Mpwapwa, as he was too much of a burden on the caravan.

For Stanley it was a most satisfactory afternoon. He had been able to make his speech and also get rid of the two weakest links in his expedition.

I was quite determined to pack it all in. I told myself I would rather die in the wilderness than suffer the same fate as Farquhar. For the first time in my life, the word "dignity" meant something to me.

A few days earlier I had sneaked into Stanley's tent to take a look at myself in his mirror, but I was unable to find it. He must have hidden it somewhere among his personal effects. While I was groping around in a drawer, I noticed that the tent had grown darker. Selim stood in the entranceway. I hadn't heard him coming.

"Get out before I call Stanley!"

"A pox on you, you Arab swine!"

May that man drown slowly, in some swamp worse than Makata.

My tattered shoes were my main problem. Where could I get a new pair? From Stanley? Hardly. So it was a question of walking back to Bagamoyo barefoot, like a Negro, or disappearing in the wilderness barefoot, like the cook.

Bombay was leading me briskly through a copse that could not be seen from the camp. It was getting dark, and I stumbled several times. Under a huge baobab tree standing alone on the far side of the copse, he stopped and turned to me. His face was close to mine, but it was so dark that I found it difficult to make out his expression. His eyes and the sparse teeth in his mouth flashed yellow. His breath had the dry smell of old tobacco.

"You do not leave us. Tell Stanley you are sorry. Then do not bother with him anymore. He does not need you. He has eaten you. You are only a shell. Listen to me. I fill you again."

I wasn't used to being consoled, and I burst into tears. Never before had I heard Bombay utter so many words in one go. As I looked up, I saw how the baobab's branches—or roots?—burned with a yellow flame against the black sky.

Bombay led me back. He held my wrist to prevent me from stumbling. He himself was able to see in the dark, like a great cat.

I don't want to die. I want to see the rhinoceroses copulating, the elephants gathering by the thousands. I want to see the whales in Lake Tanganyika. At least I want a new pair of shoes, and I want to see my mother one last time.

Bombay fetched Stanley, who, with a show of reluctance, followed him to the camp entrance. Selim lit their way with a torch. I threw myself on the ground at his feet and begged for mercy and forgiveness. At first Stanley was irritated and impatient and just wanted to get rid of me as soon as possible. He kicked me in the head. I wrapped my arms around his legs and pleaded and whined, promising to mend my ways. This improved his mood somewhat, and he started holding forth about my weakness and lack of willpower, about how magnificently patient he had been with me, about my lack of pride and manliness. Morally I was a cretin who had to be led by the hand. I had not been a good example for the Negroes. He claimed that Selim despised me.

It seemed as if I lay there for a long time. When he put the heel of his boot on my head, I understood that the ceremony was drawing to an end. I was none too comfortable lying there with my arms around his calves.

When at last he squashed my face into the mud, I almost panicked. At the same time, laughter started bubbling in my chest again, and I tried to make it sound like weeping. Stanley did not suspect. He kicked me in the neck and told me to get up. The sinner had received absolution.

He hugged me, pinched my cheeks, laughed. Finally I could release my own laughter. That was the greatest relief. We walked back through the camp with our arms around each other's shoulders, and back in his tent he poured me some British gin.

Bombay's yellow eyes had been watching us all the time.

The days are one interminable stretch of white moments.

No one waves the flies away from the small children's eyes and mouths.

Everyone sits or stands on the small dark spot that is his own shadow.

Thunder, a suckling landscape. The razor-sharp

grasses make a dry hissing sound, but deep down below our feet run subterranean rivers. The trees know them.

Everything is old. The landscape is continuous with itself, immersed in its own inaccessibility. There are no feelings here. This is not a landscape of which one can say that it is ugly or beautiful.

Somewhere out there is a watering hole where the animals congregate. Antelope and zebras make way for hyenas and wild dogs that make way for lions and rhinoceroses. Then all of them slowly leave the water's edge: the elephants are coming.

When I left Stanley's tent that evening, drums were throbbing in the distance. Where did the sound come from?

Bombay was standing in front of my tent, silent and black. I raised my lantern to his face, and the pale yellow light washed over old tarred wood. His murderer's eyes scorched me.

Stanley had poured me only one shot of gin and denied my request for a new pair of shoes. And we had just walked through camp with our arms around each other.

Gradually I calmed down. My memories paraded through the tent. Mornings on the beaches of Zanzibar. Ships on the sound. The friendly milling of people in the bazaars. Her soft navel. The sea one sunny day with a gentle breeze. Mother's apron. The mild hours in Bagamoyo when Farquhar and I sat sewing canvas under the mango tree. The blessed emptiness.

In slow motion, like a priest giving communion, I took out my rifle and loaded it. I checked all the moving parts, straightened out my clothing, combed my hair, arranged all my things carefully. Once again I regretted the mirror. Then I extinguished the lantern and stepped out into the night. I could smell the latrine, hear the distant drums.

I lay down on the ground facing Stanley's tent. He still had a small light on, and the tent gave off an incandescent glow. Shadows cast patterns over the canvas. I knew which corner his bed occupied, and took my time calculating the height of the bed and the position of the body on it. Then I adjusted my grip on the rifle and took careful aim.

The light went out, and I decided to count to twenty.

At fifteen, I panicked. I rushed back to my tent, threw the rifle in a corner, and curled up on my cot. I don't know whether I managed to fall asleep before Stanley stood at my bedside, holding a lantern.

"Shaw! Did you fire that shot?"

I assured him I hadn't fired any shots. He told me there was a bullet hole in his tent: a bullet had passed just above his head, and the sentries had confirmed that the shot came from my tent. He stuck a finger into the barrel of my rifle. When he pulled it out, it was black.

"The barrel is warm."

I remembered something that had happened a very long time ago when I was a small boy: an incredible explosion, a short but very deep silence.

"How do you explain that warm barrel? How do you explain the sentries saying that they saw you fire your rifle?"

I explained that I had seen a thief and taken a potshot at him. When Stanley shook his head, I changed the thief to a hyena, and when he went on shaking his

103

head, I said I wanted to test the rifle. Then I switched to an accidental discharge: I said that someone had tried to steal the rifle and it had gone off when I grabbed it back. I ended up saying that I thought it was Bombay who had fired the shot.

Why did I say all those things?

He sat down next to me on the cot, raised his lantern, examined my eyes. With thumb and index finger he pulled up my eyelid and looked right into my eye. His hands were soft and gentle.

"Never fire that thing at night again. You could hurt yourself."

After dismissing the sentries, he ran his palm over my forehead and said that I should try to get some sleep. Everything would turn out all right in the end. He would take care of me. He would not leave me with Farquhar.

He sat with me until I fell asleep. I had no sense of his being a living person.

When I woke up the following morning I felt lighter than ever, yet every muscle in my body ached.

We marched on. This was the hottest day so far. I lay on the donkey's back, and my sweat ran slowly down into my eyes and over my lips. It stung and tasted salty. Behind my closed eyelids I saw one white sun after another move from right to left.

Antelope and gnu were standing by puddles in dried-out riverbeds and under shady trees. A big boulder—no, a rhinoceros. A pair of lions lay panting under an acacia. None of the animals moved. The heat was their protection.

Just before Mpwapwa's slopes and heights, the thunderclouds mounted like black pillars of smoke, driving a strong wind before them. The animals raised their heads. The porters lengthened their steps. Then came a becalmed silence. The animals stood up, and the porters stopped and listened, openmouthed. A hissing wall of silvery rain approached. Everyone prepared himself to receive it. Then we were in the downpour. Trails became creeks, and the hard red clay turned to mud.

Afterward: Cool air, flowing sinuously down the windpipe to distribute its crystals in the body. From the trees fell waterdrops bigger than pearls. The puddles reflected the cleansed landscape, each shape receiving its upside-down twin.

Hearing was a knife blade. Taste, a child's tongue.

I have an itch in my armpits, in my crotch, and between my toes. Flaming heat rash is spreading into a map of proliferating islands and peninsulas. My groin is sore from riding. I have a burning sensation when I urinate, and my stool is colorless. I am also beginning to lose the battle against the dust fleas that infest our campgrounds and the villages. Saburi used to be good at picking them out of my toes with a sharp thorn. Now I have to take care of them myself. The fleas build small white nests under my toenails. The itch is worst at night.

Every night I have an attack of the chills.

But I am not getting any lighter. Sometimes I think I'm swelling up like Farquhar.

* * *

While we climbed the slopes around Mpwapwa, I found myself a short distance ahead of the rest of the caravan. For the first time, I stood by the roadside and watched it file past, until it was time for me to take up my vulnerable position in the rear.

It was a horrifying assemblage of human beings that passed before me. The deserters who had been shackled instead of flogged, on Bombay's orders, looked like the most pitiful slaves. The porters and soldiers were emaciated. A dangerous fire burned in the gaze of some, while others stared with empty, unseeing eyes. All were gray with dirt, and many limped, their loincloths tattered, their stench hard to endure. Our caravan looked like a mob of refugees without any particular destination. Remarkably, the women and children seemed to have survived the ordeal best. But the impression was deceptive: many a night my sleep had been broken by lamentations over a child's corpse.

How had my fate become linked with this herd? Does any of it make sense?

Only three men seem untouched by the hardships: Stanley, Bombay, and our guide, Hamadi. You could throw Hamadi to hungry lions and he'd still find something to joke about.

The Bearer is not touched by our journey. He *is* our journey.

In the villages it is always the children and the very old women who attract my attention. The children's spindly legs support smooth, swollen bellies. When they run, they take fast short steps so their bellies won't suffer any unnecessary motion. They burst into tears as suddenly as they stop crying again.

The old women always stand to the side and rarely pay any attention to us strangers. Yet sometimes a few come forward and stare at me unabashedly. Their reaction is always the same. My light skin strikes them like a bullet, right between the eyes, and their already lined faces explode into thousands of little wrinkles. From their toothless mouths issues a nasty, cold laughter that chills me. I get a vague sense of having exposed myself in public.

I wish those hags wouldn't laugh at me.

For several days I avoided Farquhar. I couldn't stand looking at his face. With his red eyes, his sparse, light eyebrows, and his distended skin, he looked like a fat boar ready for slaughter.

The day before we left him, he called my name from his tent. I sent a messenger to find out what he wanted. He just wanted to chat with me. I sent the messenger back to ask what he wanted to chat about. The mere thought of sitting there exchanging small talk with that monster made me feel queasy. The messenger returned with word that he just wanted to see me, his only friend.

In his misfortune and decline he tried to cling to me. In the past he had been able to condescend to me as my superior; now he wanted to suffocate me with his bloated body. He demanded compassion. Who can afford the luxury of compassion on an expedition such as ours?

Stanley heard Farquhar's cries and summoned me. When he understood that I absolutely did not want to see Farquhar again before we left him, he cheerfully offered to come with me. When I declined, he said it was an order.

Smiling, he led me into Farquhar's musty tent. I stared at the ground while Stanley held forth about endurance and readiness to sacrifice. Finally he asked whether Farquhar needed anything. After a long silence Farquhar replied that he wanted me to look into his eyes one last time. Stanley told me to do so. But I deceived them both. I looked *through* his eyes. There I saw a poisonous mudhole covered by green slime and white scum. In the middle was a shade of blue. The blue was a thin film of water slowly drying up.

"You're a coward!" Farquhar roared, and I felt as if something was about to explode in my throat. I don't know whether it was laughter or tears.

Stanley chortled:

"He is a coward, and a madman as well."

Stanley was in such a good mood that he sent for a bottle of British gin. I knocked back a large glassful, and Farquhar, who was awash in sweat, finished up half the bottle. Stanley made another speech, a farewell address to Farquhar, in which he praised the latter's merits. Farquhar involuntarily punctuated the speech with burps and short, merry fusillades of farting that ill accorded with his appearance and state of health.

Fifteen minutes later I had to vomit. Alcohol no longer agrees with me. The tropics can change a man in the most astonishing ways.

As we were breaking camp the next morning, I heard Farquhar's voice at a distance. Once again he was calling me from the hut that had been chosen as his final home.

As we marched away, his voice grew fainter and fainter. I rejoiced in the knowledge that it would soon fall silent forever. But the voice did not die away. It had built itself a nest in my ears, just as the dust fleas have done in my toes. And there it lived on, like a nagging pain, a pulsating ache in my ear. Night and day, every hour, every minute. It didn't give me a second's peace. I lost the sense of my name. It was no longer "Shaw" I heard, but a hissing sound that turned into a dark and mournful cry.

Sometimes it sounded like a bird of the forest, sometimes like a jackal's howl. In the end I heard my name every time a wild beast opened its mouth.

I did not sleep at night. I hated.

The Interior

Time is transparent and as unchangeable as glass. It does not move. I do, slowly.

Stanley throws his sticks. I run to fetch them. No one expects the dog to comment on the ridiculous game afterward.

I want my writing to be heavy, like the drums at night, like when the soldiers throw a live pig onto the butchering block, heavy as the shade of the mango tree.

But the words are pulverized, diluted, turned into gas. First they become light and opaque like the morning fog. Then, as the warmth of the sun cautiously advances its tongue, they dissolve without resistance. What remains is a mute, altogether terrible day of heat, dirt, and horror. Where did the words go?

Perhaps that is how it should be.

Stanley claims that the whole world is following our expedition in thought, concern, and prayer. I know they are not doing that in Bagamoyo, much less in Simbamwenni. They're still cursing us in Kingaru. In Zanzibar, Dr. Kirk, the British consul, probably thinks about us now and again. But in Europe and America, according to Stanley, millions are following us. It must have something to do with the distance. The greater the distance, the greater the interest. Just the opposite of what you'd ordinarily expect. Our expedition is extraordinary.

I am a child again. Often my breast fills with the same stillness a child may feel in a strange place.

I record in order to erase. Writing is the most exact instrument for forgetting. Saburi did not know how to write. He had to carry our shared memory.

Many years ago, I was on a ship with a sailor who had an unusual pastime. He took small caged birds out to sea with him. When the ship had reached its farthest point from dry land, he released the birds and stood staring after them for a long time as they wheeled out and disappeared across the boundless expanse of water. Hardly any of them came back to the ship.

The sailor would then brood endlessly over those birds, whether they reached land or were swallowed up by the waves when they grew tired, whether they stuck together or lost each other in the salt-laden winds.

"And now they're all alone out at sea," he would say mournfully.

Our caravan has joined two other caravans. Like three tributaries, we have come together to form one huge river of more than four hundred people. We are a nation, moving along, erecting small cities, societies that come into being for a few days and then disappear. There are times when I fall in love with a campsite. In one afternoon you can become deeply attached to the few square feet of ground on which your tent is pitched. In a few seconds, you can come to hate the very same patch of ground.

The two other caravans are led by Arabs, Thani and Hamed. They're carrying cloth and other desirable goods from Zanzibar to Unyanyembe. On the way back they'll be transporting ivory or slaves or both.

Thani is just what I've imagined an Arab should be: calm, thoughtful, and possessed of a slow, steady cunning. He is tall, thin, and dark-skinned. His back is as curved as his nose.

Hamed is his opposite: restless and impulsive, too much a victim of his sudden whims to be truly deceitful. Physically, too, he contrasts with Thani: he is short and chubby, and his skin is light and soft as a baby's. He is always in a sweat.

The two of them balance each other out. Stanley respects but hates Thani, despises but loves Hamed. He doesn't understand Thani for one moment but understands Hamed only too well.

Slowly the combined caravan rolls across the Wagogos' fiery plains, confident and secure despite—or perhaps because—its leaders' continuous wrangling over routes, campsites, speed of travel. It's as if their quarreling gives the caravan its required nourishment. And the more they bicker, the more likely they are to leave the rest of us alone.

Thani's cautious line always emerges victorious, since Stanley's and Hamed's instincts are inevitably at odds. As soon as Thani senses that he is being outmaneuvered, he capitulates with an inscrutable look. The other two then become uncertain and call on Bombay to decide the whole thing. Although Bombay doesn't know who has advocated what, he always sides with Thani, and that's that. Bombay's words are boulders rolling into Stanley's tent.

Thus, Stanley has been neutralized. He has given up his commander-in-chief airs and now pretends to be an experienced leader of caravans. Repeated bouts of fever lay him low, and Selim looks after him as if he were a child. Every time he falls ill, four or perhaps even five hundred men, women, and children have to make camp and wait for his recovery. Thani does not mind waiting. He enjoys his food and his women. He even plays with his children. Hamed, on the other hand, is always about to burst. He whines and complains that Stanley's ailments are ruining him. Other caravans using faster routes are beating him to the market in Unyanyembe. On several occasions he has lost patience and started out with his people in the middle of the night, only to return late the following morning. Fear of attack by the warlike Wagogos has always caused him to turn around.

I enjoy sitting in Stanley's tent listening to the interminable disputes. As often as not, Stanley is lying on his bed, pale and feverish, with Selim by his side. Thani is sitting on a rug, and Hamed is pacing back and forth, angry and upset. Thani laughs, a slow African laugh, and likes to talk about things unrelated to caravan business. He'll sleep on it, postpone the decision, being of the opinion that many problems solve themselves. Often he asks Stanley and me about Europe. He is a very knowledgeable man.

Hamed always argues for immediate departure and the straightest possible route.

Finally Stanley tries to come up with daring and surprising solutions, but these mostly come down to ways to avoid paying tribute to the chief.

They are like half-grown children. For Stanley, the caravan is a toy to be cuddled one moment and thrown against the wall the next, in a sudden fit of rage. Hamed is the grouchy, perpetually aggrieved fat boy. Thani is the lazy, pampered chap in his teens who gets everything just by pointing his finger.

But the more Thani's cautious approach determines our progress, the swifter our caravan seems to proceed. I am content.

Hamed has continual discipline problems with his people. His wives and female slaves scream and throw pots at him, his porters and soldiers sit down and refuse to budge, demanding better pay. All of this is due to his capricious leadership. Stanley avails himself of every opportunity to sneer at his lack of authority.

One afternoon there was a steady drizzle. Everybody was resting in tents or makeshift shelters. I sat in Stanley's tent, just inside the entrance, and looked out at the gray, scarcely visible rain, which made a low hissing noise on the tent canvas. Stanley lay prostrate on his bed, like a delicate young lady of noble birth. Thani reclined on a couple of cushions, and even Hamed had come to rest on a cushion. I was enjoying the idle moments. Hamed was suffering. Stanley was moody after a couple of days of fever and busy worrying about the coming encounter with the Sultan in Mvumi, who was notorious for demanding exorbitant tribute. Thani had closed his eyes and was humming some monotonous melody.

Hamed opened up his heart:

"My porters do not obey me. Not even my youngest wife obeys me. A young slave girl kicked me out last night when I came to her bed to enjoy her. And no one will buy my goods in Unyanyembe. They already have all they need. Allah has abandoned me."

"Stop fretting," said Thani in a consoling tone. "Your women love you, and the buyers are waiting for you in Unyanyembe."

After a moment's silence, Stanley's weak voice came from the bed.

"My men always obey me."

"But if they do not, what do you do?"

"Flog 'em."

"And if that does not work?"

"Shoot 'em."

Thani shook his head, his eyes still closed.

"My friend, you are too hard. It is better to slaughter a goat and let them have a feast. After that, they will obey. And a goat is cheaper to replace than a dead man."

Hamed pondered.

"I promise them money, and sometimes I pay them what I promise, when we get to our destination. That works—sometimes."

Stanley came to life and sat up. He waved his arm in

the direction of the deep, fast-running river right next to our campsite.

"I could order my men to cross at the deepest point, carrying full loads."

"But why?" Thani opened one eye.

Hamed's eyes flashed, his lips formed a smile. He threw out his net, certain of a catch.

"I do not believe for one moment that they would obey you. If you shoot one of them, the others will rebel. I am prepared to wager a goat that you cannot manage that."

"No wagers! I believe you, Stanley!"

But Thani's appeal was in vain. I had to go out into the rain to fetch Bombay. On our way back to the tent I gave him a quick summary of the situation.

"That must not happen," he said glumly.

Stanley gave him the order: the entire caravan was to break camp and get ready to cross the river, carrying full loads, at the deepest and most turbulent point.

Bombay listened, his face expressionless. After a while he said that the result would simply be that Hamed would lose a goat and Stanley would be forced to endure a hardship his body was not yet ready for. He would also lose some of his best men. Bombay assured the two Arabs that in the end Stanley would succeed in driving the men through the rapids, but no one would be served by this. Therefore, he proposed a compromise: he would have a kid slaughtered, to be paid for by both Hamed and Stanley. The kid would then be prepared as a feast for the three caravan leaders.

Stanley and Hamed looked at each other out of the corners of their eyes. Then they nodded their assent, and Thani said with relief:

"Bombay, if you were an Arab, I would make you my partner."

"If I were an Arab, I would not need a partner," Bombay replied, and left the tent.

Stanley looked furious, but Thani waved a pacifying hand.

"It is Allah who has made him intelligent. Nothing we can do about it. Besides, he has made up for his impertinence by arranging that feast for me. You see, I'm the only one who has gained anything from your wager."

Such conversations and incidents entertained me greatly. They didn't really concern my own life. I feel safe with the Arabs. Even Hamed knows his limits. He is too miserly to kill and too cowardly to be foolhardy. When the situation becomes insufferable, they just lie down and eat or go to their women—Thani lazily and absentmindedly, Hamed furiously, like an aroused wild boar. After all, it is Allah who guides the mainstream of life.

Stanley has issued me a new pair of shoes. The joy I felt when I put them on made me worry about the state of my sanity.

At night, I dream about her soft navel. These are adolescent dreams that make me believe I have a future.

Why shouldn't I be able to lead a caravan and trade between Bagamoyo and Unyanyembe, just like Thani and Hamed? Get some porters and soldiers, a few female slaves, and employ Bombay as my captain. Travel to Zanzibar a couple of times a year and meet old friends and new in the bazaars, get drunk for a few days, buy provisions, and then return to the interior.

I'd be admired and respected, perhaps even loved and feared. If Stanley decides to undertake another expedition to Ujiji, he'll get in touch with me, seek my advice, then ask me if I will consider taking charge of his caravan. My advice he shall have, but I'll refuse the partnership offer with a friendly laugh; I couldn't dream of taking part in an expedition without being solely responsible for it.

None of it is all that improbable. The principle is amazingly simple: you buy cloth, thread, glass beads, and so on, and then sell them in the interior. With the profit you purchase ivory (and slaves, everybody does) to sell on the coast. Your wealth keeps growing, and you invest in buildings, ships, farms, and new caravans. Not that improbable. Buy low in one place, sell high in another. What could be simpler?

I am strong. Even Stanley has noticed how well I am. He's investing in me. Not only have I received a pair of new shoes but a pair of trousers and a shirt as well. Last night he offered me a glass of gin and conversed with me almost as if I were his equal. It is not unthinkable that we may understand each other better from now on.

I only wish I didn't find it so hard to fall asleep. The ghost of poor Farquhar still haunts me. Deep inside my ear rises a soft hissing that swells into a protracted wail. The sound echoes from the throats of the wilderness, I start and sit up on my cot. All around the camp, all over the wilderness, this sound is heard, sometimes a roar, sometimes a mournful call, sometimes a short howl. Sha-a-a-w.

Before I fall asleep it seems that the day's happy moods were merely borrowed. The cry within my ear and in the wilderness tells me that all things will pass, even my well-being. Soon I shall be dazzled by the white light of truth.

Is it worth struggling? Can one defy one's fate? What could Farquhar do about his fate? It wasn't my fault that we were compelled to leave him there, screaming and miserable. I can't help it that his throat was torn by the same sound that rolls from the beasts of the wilderness. My name.

The skin on my arms is yellow. I had thought it would grow darker in the sun. It looks as if I had washed myself in urine.

A few days ago I saw a herd of gnu. I didn't know such ugly creatures existed in Africa; they look like a cross between an elk, a horse, and a cow. By itself, a gnu is a monstrosity. Its sloping back and grotesquely flattened head made me think it was an herbivorous relative of the hyena. But in a herd, seen at a distance, these creatures have a timeless beauty. In full flight across a savannah, the stiff canter of the individual animal dissolves in the collective motion of the herd. Like flowing water or gusts of wind across a grassy plain, they move along on their constant migrations. There's hardly another animal that is as much a part of the savannah. The herd instinct of the gnu is the savannah's soul.

I am happy. My life rests in a cool, shady bird's nest where the flickering light of the sun sometimes reaches me through the dense foliage. Right next to me is a great ticking heart. I am so happy that I can sense the smell of the water and hear the gliding flight of the clouds. Colorful butterflies wing their way into and out of my head. I float along on a pleasantly warm and humid wave of air.

One day Stanley summoned me. He stood waiting in the shade of a mango tree. I was to be given an important task. He put his arm around my shoulders, and we walked a few steps.

"You will give me a haircut. I can't trust any of these Negroes to do it. Thank God my hair isn't frizzy like theirs. And I don't trust Selim either, not in this matter. Who knows how these Arabs wear their hair under those fezzes and turbans."

We were camped on a lovely site, a hillside. We had fresh water and shade from both mangoes and palms. The village just below our camp was inhabited by a friendly, handsome people who sold us food at low prices. Their women were so pretty that the porters and soldiers refrained from their customary uncouth behavior.

Right by the mango tree, where Selim had placed a chair, ran a stream with clear water. The shrubbery around the stream was alive with small songbirds, and a little farther down, where the stream widened onto a sandy beach, naked children were bathing while their slender mothers waded in to fetch water. They rolled up their skirts, and the water reached up to their shiny black thighs. When they had filled their jars, they slowly waded back, chatting and laughing.

My happiness unfolded like a flower.

Looking down, I saw Stanley's boyish neck, his hair grown long over it. Something gave inside me, and I felt tenderness for that neck. My inner peace was undisturbed by Stanley's irritable voice as he chased off the spectators who had gathered around us. Only Thani and Hamed stayed for a moment's entertainment. Through my fingertips on his hair I sensed that he hated those two.

A dark memory flitted through my head like the shadow of a flying bird: a neighbor boy from my childhood street, ugly, dirty, and vicious, his face like a distorted reflection in a convex mirror. Snot drips from his nostrils, and he is drooling. His hair is in ragged tufts, as if someone had torn it out by the roots.

My happy hands started work of their own accord. I was somewhere else. Stanley shifted in his seat. Thani and Hamed came closer, curiosity in their eyes. They exchanged a glance that showed something was amiss. Stanley got up quickly and sent Selim to fetch his mirror. I ran my hand over the knobbly skull, which looked as if it could use some consolation. He struck it aside and cursed. Thani retreated a bit, turning his back. Hamed laughed openly, like a fool.

When Stanley raised the looking-glass, I leaned forward and peered over his shoulder, hoping to see my own reflection. I had just caught a glimpse of a gray-flecked beard when Stanley turned and struck me over the head with the mirror with all his might. The glass splintered and shimmered like a kaleidoscope in the yellow afternoon sunlight before it hit the ground. I felt no pain.

Stanley screamed for Selim, who ran to the tent and

came back with Bombay. Selim gave Stanley a skullcap, and he quickly slapped it on his head.

My mouth started talking of its own accord.

"I didn't know you were Jewish."

The two Arabs rushed off, biting their hands. Only Bombay remained, and his ebony face cracked into a horrifying laugh that frightened me for a second.

"Selim! The donkey whip!"

Laughing hysterically, I ran for the stream and dove in fully clothed. The beautiful women fled the water, their sinuous charms bathed in liquid cascades. Like monkeys, the children clambered into the branches that hung above the stream.

On the other side I sat down on a fallen tree, panting, and saw Stanley wielding the whip.

"I did my best!"

"Come back and take your punishment."

The situation took an unexpected turn. The women gathered around me, laughing and commiserating: they dried my face, pulled my clothes off without inhibition, and wrapped me in a colorful cloth. They squealed when they saw my white, uncircumcised member and pinched me here and there. I felt the firm breasts of a young woman against my back, and as I struggled to keep my balance, I took hold of another woman's soft upper arm. They smelled of sweet water, earth, smoke, and something slightly acid. I wished they were all my wives.

Across the stream, Stanley had calmed himself. He sat down again, and Selim shaved his head. His bare skull was the same color as a white man's corpse. When Selim was done, Stanley put on his favorite peaked cap and disappeared into his tent. He kept wearing that cap until his hair grew out again.

And of this event, though it was perhaps the most beautiful of our journey, Stanley never said another word.

Stanley is bald, ill, and afraid of dying. It is hard to tell whether Selim is apprehensive or pleased.

We camp out in paradise and wait for him to get well. Hamed tears his hair and beats his women. Thani meditates and enjoys his women. Every day he talks things over with Stanley and Hamed, then makes his decisions in consultation with Bombay.

I am kept informed.

Every conversation among the porters and soldiers ends with a comment about "the whirlwind," "the mighty voice," "the strong spear": Mirambo, chief of the bloodthirsty Wagogos and enemy of gentle Mkasiwa, chief of wealthy and coveted Unyanyembe. Only Stanley poohpoohs such talk.

We're on our way again, to the heart of Unyanyembe: Tabora. The other day we encountered an amiable slave trader on his way to the coast with a train of newly captured slaves. He promised to look after Farquhar and even take him to the coast, if possible. My treachery opened up like an internal wound. I hastened to wrap my female figurine in a pretty cloth and entrust it to the trader as a gift to Farquhar.

There are few deeds I have regretted so much. I don't understand why I did it. Farquhar doesn't need it, it means nothing to him; in his eyes it's just a piece of wood shaped like a woman. I regretted it the minute it left my hand. It left an absolute void, a small volume of nothing. This emptiness moves around me during the days. At night it lies at the bottom of my trunk, except when it crawls out and tries to enter my mouth and suffocate me.

But for that void, I would be the happiest man in the world.

Right now I am sitting here writing in Kwihara, not far from Tabora. We have stopped here for a longer stay, and our expedition enters a new phase. The Arabs have put a large house at Stanley's disposal, and I have been assigned a small room, just as in Bagamoyo.

The place is teeming with rich Arabs. But there are even more in Tabora, thousands of them living in great luxury. They own many slaves and employ them to cultivate the huge plain surrounding the town. They grow rice, sweet potatoes, maize, millet, peas, sesame, and farther out on the plain they keep herds of cows and goats that provide meat, milk, and butter. They sell ivory and slaves in Zanzibar and buy cloth, spices, and all the requisites of the good life. Every male Arab has a harem to satisfy his lusts and bear him sons, as well as servants and slaves both male and female. Every man is a king in his kingdom.

Stanley is childishly flattered by their attentions. They visit him humbly and invite him to lavish banquets. They send him black slave girls whom he waves off brusquely, his voice thick, his gaze frightened, his hand hard. I caught one young girl on her way back from Stanley, her mission incomplete, and took her quickly and joylessly. Her passive body was so full of disdain that her eyes and loins brought tears to my eyes. Why am I not hard enough?

Bombay worries me. Something has happened to him. Sometimes the darkness of the night flows out of him, sometimes his murderer's face is radiant with an inner sun. He is the only one who must not change.

I haven't had a fever for two weeks, and it has done me good to take a break from riding. The sores on my groin got better in only a few days. However, I am now afflicted with boils on my legs. Walking exhausts me, and I break into a sweat as soon as I move. It is remarkable that all the hardships have not caused me to lose weight. Surely it is easier to inhabit a small, slender body than a large one. Saburi's skinny little body was perfect for the plains of Africa.

What I remember best of the journey from Bagamoyo are the happy moments: to hold my member lightly, gently baring the tip, to feel the cool wind on its damp, soft head and then the urine streaming forth, to tuck it back into my trousers as if it were a small animal that liked to bask in the sun or slowly glide through warm, flowing water.

Although I've ridden most of the way, I have now learned to walk, to know my own stride: how each step resembles its thousands of predecessors; the happy anticipation in the arch of the foot, the muscles of calf and thigh, before a rock, a hole, a fallen branch; the foreknowledge of how the foot will perform; the pleasure in the step the foot is about to take.

When we pass through dense foliage, spiderwebs often cling to my face. I usually brush the sticky strands away with a laugh. I don't know why I always laugh when I do that.

A couple of weeks before our arrival in Kwihara, we were robbed—that's Stanley's term—by a powerful sultan. He kept demanding more and more tribute, and Bombay would trudge off, mute as a stone, carrying one heavy load after another. Hamed wept. Stanley shouted, swore revenge, urged violent action. He called his Arab partners cowardly Asiatics and spineless women. They weren't fazed. Thani's face grew long and equine and took on a color resembling Bombay's.

There was nothing to be done. Both Thani and Bombay knew that an open battle would have ended in our annihilation.

Everybody spoke of this as a catastrophe. That was a lie. They were merely compelled to pay three times as much as they themselves thought reasonable. Their capital was intact. It wasn't so much the cost that upset them as the feeling of having been had.

My hopes of seeing my reflection are gone. Stanley's looking glass was shattered against my head. I'm sure the Arab women have mirrors, but I'm afraid to approach them. No strangers are allowed near them.

Above all I would like to see my eyes. When I look out over the enormous plain around Kwihara it feels as if my eyes were fading away. It feels as if they were taking on the same watery blue that you see in the eyes of really old English sailors—the same color, by the way, as Farquhar's eyes on the day we left him. His red pig's eyes changed overnight.

My muscles are occupied by a squadron of army ants. The troops march about in the loose-fitting shell while the sea washes in through the eyes.

Only a few hours ago Stanley came into my room whistling shrilly and tunelessly. Beaming, he declared that he had decided to go to war against Mirambo! Instantly I felt a spear pierce my neck and strike the most vulnerable part of my brain. Stanley goes merrily whistling into battle against the most powerful and warlike sultan in the interior of Africa!

It is all the Arabs' fault. They saw how vain and belligerent Stanley was and invited him to extravagant banquets, in the course of which they toasted him as the most remarkable man who had ever come to Unyanyembe. During one of these feasts, Stanley "happened"—his word—to become part of a war council in which he was treated to an eloquent description of the situation in the region: Mirambo has closed the trade route between Tabora and Ujiji and is threatening to wipe out the Arab colonies and make the gentle Sultan of Unyanyembe his vassal. All decent men must come to the rescue, and if Stanley wants to get to Ujiji, it will be wise for him to help open that caravan route again. Stanley lapped it all up like a camel drinking water.

So now we shall go to war by the side of the slave traders, against a man who is a horrifying combination of war-crazed tyrant and beloved defender of freedom.

With infallible precision Stanley walks into every difficulty that presents itself in our vicinity. The only thing that may save him in this case is that he does not seem to believe it will be a real war. Is it possible to die in a make-believe war?

It pains me that I have suddenly become so insightful. It had never occurred to me before that seeing through things can cause such anxiety. I have to talk to Bombay. Analysis and strategy are not my strong suits.

How can a man like Stanley, whose whole life has been built on common sense and decisiveness, think so shallowly and act so superficially? His thoughts are a straight road that is compelled to do battle with everything it crosses. Just now that road goes to the center of Africa, which is inhabited by Arabs and by Mirambo. He is so suggestible. To him the world is just a map to draw lines on. Like a river running upstream, he is forced to hurl himself at every obstacle. What is the magnet that pulls him through his troubles? Sometimes I think his imprudence hides a profound intuition. Perhaps he doesn't need a boat; perhaps he can walk on water?

Bombay is allowing Stanley to take a small band of soldiers to the war. Most of them will stay here in Kwihara to guard our camp. The porters have been paid off and are no longer in Stanley's employ. I have been chosen for combat. Should I laugh or should I weep? The closest I've ever been to battle was a saloon fight I witnessed in Amsterdam where a rowdy sailor was stabbed.

I am surprised by Bombay's attitude to the war. When I tried to convince him that Stanley had been hoodwinked by the Arabs, he just shook his head.

"It is Mirambo who deceives them all."

"But why are you going?"

"To get close to Mirambo."

"But you may be killed."

"It is no shame to be killed by Mirambo."

Shame? Maybe. I don't give a damn for shame or glory. This war is suicide.

Stanley summoned me yesterday. I found him in his bathroom; the one here in Kwihara is much better appointed than the one in Bagamoyo where I took my compulsory bath. He said nothing, merely registered my arrival. I sat down and watched while he washed and shaved. He turned to me only after he had put on a dazzling white linen shirt. I was ready for the customary exhortations on the importance of good hygiene. Outward cleanliness is a mirror of the state of the soul, he always said. But instead:

"Come with me. We shall pray together."

At first I wasn't sure I had heard right, but he took me to his bedroom and got down on his knees by the bed, indicating that I should do the same. Then, in a high-pitched staccato, he recited this prayer:

"God help us in the task that lies before us. Help us crush the heathen tyrant Mirambo, help us spread Thy light and our civilization over this dark continent, in word and deed. Amen."

That was that. He dismissed me with a wave of the hand.

"I didn't know you believed in God."

He looked at me, uncomprehending.

"Don't ever forget that we are white men, Shaw! May that heathen Mirambo's testicles burn in hell!" (A phrase he must have picked up from the Arabs.)

I left his dark bedroom and stepped out into the glaring sunlight of the hot, dusty courtyard. I took the step from a cool barracks where minutes and seconds ticked away among maps and notations, into a stifling white heat where time was a scrawny chicken that had scratched itself a place in the shade of a bush. It was gasping through open beak and blinking slowly with its lower eyelids.

How can Stanley stand all these rituals?

My bowel movements are now in phase with the sun and moon. They offer a slow, pleasurable resistance, as if they wanted to stretch out the day's motions and stop the implacable progress of the heavenly bodies in a happy paean to all foul-smelling forces of disintegration.

I haven't had diarrhea since I cut Stanley's hair.

While I've shrunk some, I feel more solid than ever before. It is as if someone had poured molten steel into this pitiful, pale, sweaty, fatty shell that is my outward form.

The only discordant element is Farquhar's cry, multiplying itself to infinity in the wilderness. How does he manage it? If Saburi were alive, he might be able to tell me. It is still a long hissing sound, followed by a low mournful one: *Sha-a-a-w!* When I wake up at night to urinate, it terrifies me. I can feel it in my teeth.

* * *

I had thought that nothing, absolutely nothing, could surprise me anymore, yet I am as astonished as a child. The world can still change, take wonderful or frightening turns.

Bombay has fallen in love. Now I know that a boulder can love the clear brook that caresses its base. The clear brook, in this case, is not only Unyanyembe's most corpulent female, she is also that town's wealthiest businesswoman and its most notorious sorceress. When Bombay launched his hatchet of a gaze at her shiny fat face, she waved her arm in a sweeping gesture and shooed the parasitic admirers out of her store, which was filled to the rafters with bric-a-brac. Presto, she became—a clear rivulet, an adolescent girl with a body bursting with giggles and budding charms.

Now Bombay visits her house every night, and if the gifts she showers upon him are any indication, she must appreciate his murderous energy and devastating masculinity.

This woman, whose name is Mama Simba, was sold into slavery on the West Coast, finally bought her freedom, and now presides over a network of businesswomen and businessmen who distribute the Arabs' goods all over Unyanyembe. She even trades with Mirambo's people. She is the middleman between the poor Negro and the wealthy Arab. As much of her trade is barter, she owns huge stores of basic necessities, which she resells to caravans and other buyers. Despite her wealth, she has wisely refrained from competing with the Arabs, accepting the fact that her position depends on their business activities.

I can't really explain why Bombay's love affair pleases me so. Of course I am glad for his sake, but that's not the main reason. Bombay is not the sort of man with whom it is easy to empathize. Maybe it's just because it was such a surprise.

When Bombay passed by my window a little while ago, like a thundercloud on its way to pour its waters over parched ground, I stood up and shouted cheap jokes after him. He didn't even hear me.

Now happy events are occurring in rapid succession. It's almost disquieting: can I accept them? Old humiliations lie in my chest like hard balls and resist.

Suddenly—Bombay always appears suddenly—he stood there, casting his shadow over me. With a deep bark he urged me to follow him. I stopped what I was doing, and we left Kwihara on a small path I had never followed before. The choice of route made me realize that we were on an unusual errand.

Leaving the great plain, we proceeded through mountainous terrain with dense vegetation around ravinelike gorges. After marching for over an hour we arrived at a fork in the path, and Bombay stopped and told me to wait there. He disappeared down one of the paths and left me alone, a fact that struck me with unexpected force. I could hear the sound of running water in the distance, and a band of chattering monkeys went by. A forest bird uttered a chilling cry. I thought about leopards and snakes, of which there were surely plenty in these wooded mountains. After a while I noticed that I'd been standing too close to a parade of army ants that were breaking ranks to crawl up my legs and bite them. As I was stamping and slapping at them, I glimpsed a shadow behind me and to one side. I spun around and stood face to face with—Bombay. When he saw my fright, a glimmer of amusement showed in the black and yellow eyes and on his wide, thick lips.

What happened after that I remember as one remembers a dream: there are details of an almost painful clarity, but the narrative is disrupted by gaps in memory and inexplicable episodes. Bombay made sure that we were alone; that frightened me. Were we being pursued? He put an index finger to his lips to indicate that I shouldn't open my mouth. And then he said, almost whispering, but slowly and clearly to avoid having to repeat himself or being misunderstood:

"When you get in the water, keep your eyes open!"

Then he turned to look at the path down which he had vanished a little while ago, as if waiting for someone to appear. And sure enough, in a few minutes we heard the firm little steps approaching. A moment later, bouncing along heavily on a small donkey, Mama Simba appeared. As Bombay helped her down, she exuded a narcotic aroma of perfume and sweat. She gave me an absentminded little nod, as if she found it perfectly natural that we had met there.

Bombay tied the donkey to a tree, and we proceeded down the path, which led us toward the bottom of a deep gorge overgrown with dense virgin forest. Steep cliff walls rose on both sides, and the sound of running water became louder. Mama Simba swayed along ponderously, and I saw drops of sweat running down her neck.

133

In ten minutes we were there: when I saw the spot, I knew immediately that it was our destination. It was perhaps the most beautiful place I had ever seen. At the bottom of the gorge, a break in the vegetation revealed a very high waterfall descending in a soft line to a crystal-clear body of calm water. All around, steam rose from the moist greenery. The most remarkable thing was the quality of the light. The vertical cliff wall seemed incandescent, and rainbows danced in the water vapor rising from the falls. The fiery yellow cliff and the deep green of the vegetation created a light that made us feel we were indoors. The small lagoon itself was a strong light blue. The water smelled sweet, and millions of droplets covered our skin.

Bombay motioned me to take off my clothes, as he himself was doing. Slowly we descended into a fireworks display of light and water reflections that painted our bodies in rainbow stripes. The colors shone beautifully on Bombay's black, muscular body.

When he slid into the water, I did likewise. I held my nose, let my head sink under the surface, and heeded Bombay's admonition to keep my eyes open. Bubbles rose from chalk-white rocks, and small crablike creatures scuttled off to hide. The water was cool and fresh. Blue shadows moved across the glittering sandy bottom. I heard sounds that were encapsulated in a protective coating, and for a second my eyes met Bombay's fishlike killer stare.

When I surfaced again, I saw that Bombay was already getting out of the water. His long, circumcised member slapped against his wet black thighs as he climbed up onto the tender green of the lagoon's edge.

I followed him and met Mama Simba's inscrutable gaze, which had been upon us all the time.

Without a word, we dressed and departed. I felt as if I had shed twenty years. The boils on my legs had healed, and my skin felt soft as velvet. The muscles in my thighs and calves flexed pleasantly with every step, and the damp air I was inhaling in long deep draughts swirled through my chest.

We didn't stop until we reached the place where the paths converged and Mama Simba's donkey stood waiting. She turned to Bombay and asked him something that he thought over for a moment before replying. The answer seemed to please her. Then she addressed a question to me, and Bombay interpreted.

"What did you see under the water?"

"Whales."

Bombay had to repeat the question, and I had to explain. Then it took him a long time to explain my answer to Mama Simba. At last she seemed to understand.

"You will survive the war," she told me. "You won't even be wounded. Both of you will be all right."

Bombay boosted her up onto the little donkey. Obediently it started trotting away with its heavy burden. Mama Simba turned and gave a short, ringing laugh. After a while she laughed again, but this time she couldn't stop. She laughed so hard that Bombay had to support her to keep her from falling off. Bombay, too, began to laugh. It was a terrible sound, a harsh cough not unlike the warning cry of an antelope.

All the way back to Kwihara I listened to their duet: her waterfall laugh, which seemed to come from a spot just above her head, and his coughing laugh, which rumbled from his guts. I was happy. Most of all I would have liked to lie in Mama Simba's lap and feel her laughter rising through the rolls of fat on her belly and the enormous gourds of her breasts. I would have liked to enjoy her sweet and sour fragrances, the odors of her perfume, her armpits, her sex, and to feel her soft, smooth, oily arms around my body.

I was happy because they had taken me to that spring, because they cared for me.

Today, happiness lies close to the bones of my skull and bobs up and down in a puddle of unshed tears. Should the dam break, something in my chest will melt down into a small glowing bullet.

It hurts.

When one of Stanley's best soldiers, a taciturn and grave young man of Mirambo's tribe, understood that he had been chosen to take part in the war against Mirambo, he said:

"Then I will die."

And he lay down on the ground and began to fade away. The other soldiers stood in a circle around him, staring mutely, and Stanley came too, and started kicking him. When Stanley finally understood that he was about to lose his best warrior, he released him from the mission. But it was too late. The decision had been made, the spark of life extinguished.

"It is his fate," said Bombay, and made sure that no one disturbed the man.

Only twenty-four hours later the grave warrior had forced the life from his body.

Death is so near. I wish that I too had willpower.

The day before we went out to do battle, Bombay acquired a dangerous rival: Hamadi, our cheerful guide. The latter had plied his charms to make Mama Simba laugh that waterfall laugh. Smiling people flocked to her store. Nostrils flaring, Bombay took a knife and strode over there. Hamadi started screaming at the top of his lungs, but Mama Simba intervened: she bared all her good-natured avoirdupois to Bombay's knife, and he plunged it into a wall. The drama was over in a minute. Bombay cut his hand, and the people of Kwihara had something to talk about.

The war is over now. I got lighter again but am slowly swelling. Inside my body the great boulder is falling silently back into the ravine. My bath in the holy water with Bombay saved me from the least scratch during the skirmishes. My brain, on the other hand, is proceeding across the plains in all possible directions at once.

We marched out of Kwihara with the American flag snapping at the head of our column. Stanley was in the best of spirits even though Bombay had delayed our departure with a final visit to Mama Simba.

It took us three days to reach the village where the joint forces were to assemble: the well-equipped troops of the Arabs, Chief Mkasiwa's entire army, and Stanley's small force. Altogether there were over two thousand men, at least half of whom were slaves. All resources had been mobilized to put an end, once and for all, to Mirambo's plans of conquest. How could anyone resist this mighty army?

The camp was more like a marketplace than a military outpost. The rainy season notwithstanding, the plain was dry and dusty. Everyone was nervously busy: amid heat and noise, food and drink changed hands feverishly; people bartered valuables and amulets, bought courage and immortality, sacrificed cocks and sheep to the ancestors. Arab astrologers and mullahs screamed predictions and blessings over the teeming masses, who were more interested in painting their bodies with plant juices and practicing infernal war cries than in listening to prophecies of success. Ecstatic men went around promising rewards for victory, extolling the joys of plunder, and shouting their hatred of the evil Mirambo. Some offered the soldiers drugs that made them shake as if in a fever, and in the smoke from sacrificial fires, the most courageous cut bloody stripes into their cheeks, rolling their eyes so the whites showed. All this was accompanied by war drums and war dances.

Stanley forced me to walk around with him and admire this "impressive spectacle," as he called it. I thought it horrible. The noise boomed through my body as if I were a sounding board; it filled me and echoed in my inner hollows until my ears threatened to explode. I only wanted the noise to stop. I would have killed for silence.

The war became a nightmarish labyrinth, blood and guts flying everywhere, time and space constantly shifting, events that seemed drawn from distant memories suddenly materializing in front of your eyes. Some of the atrocities seemed to me more like premonitions of future catastrophes than real occurrences.

We won victories that were hardly victories, and we suffered a defeat that was much more than a defeat.

During one of the first days of the war, the joint forces surrounded a small village in which Mirambo was rumored to be staying. Our two thousand heavily armed men stormed this village of less than five hundred people, including women and children. The makeshift fortifications were trampled down, and behind them the army encountered a small group of soldiers who already wore death on their faces. They fought bravely, without joy and without hope, and were soon cut down. Spears ripped their stomachs open, and their intestines coiled out on the ground. The wounded and defenseless were blinded and castrated. At a range of one meter they were shot through the temple, and the decapitated heads were borne aloft in triumph on the points of spears. Within the village, mortally frightened women and children were making clumsy attempts to hide. The women were raped, and their wombs slit open. The children lost eyes and hands and were thrown alive into burning houses. The screams of those children had reached a pitch of terror far beyond their world.

I moved through the inferno like a sleepwalker. Afterward, I did find some bloody scratches on my back, which I assume I received when Stanley drove me into the thick of combat with his riding crop. After the battle, he led me past our blood-drenched men, intoxicated by their accomplishment, to see the Arab leaders and Sultan Mkasiwa. Greetings of manly rejoicing were exchanged and congratulations expressed on the occasion of a glorious victory. Only Mkasiwa's face was impassive.

The atrocities continued day after day. Our forces

marched from one village to the next, pillaging and killing. Mirambo's villages were swallowed up the way a starving dog devours a strip of meat. But Mirambo was nowhere to be found. Bombay, who was constantly by my side as if our fates were linked, said:

"You cannot beat Mirambo like you beat a dog. Mirambo is everywhere. He has not shown his face yet."

After one of our many victories, the army set off again in pursuit of new prizes, singing, bathed in blood from the enemy's wounds, loaded down with the spoils of war. That was when Mirambo showed his face. Suddenly his warriors were everywhere; they attacked us from all sides. I glimpsed them only for a few confused seconds. These weren't men armed as soldiers. They were born warriors, painted warriors in feather headdresses, and they attacked us with the strength of the lion, the suppleness of the panther, and the weight of the elephant. Bombay flung me on the back of my donkey and led us out of the ambush at a run. It was no fight. Our soldiers fled or gave up, cowered on the ground, bared their necks, and let themselves be slaughtered.

During our escape, one of Mirambo's warriors sprang up out of nowhere and blocked our way. He hesitated for a second at the sight of my white face, then laughed a quiet laugh, melodious but joyless. That laugh doomed him. A shot rang out next to me, and the warrior fell as if his whole life had been a preparation for death. Bombay shouldered the rifle again, and we continued our flight.

* * *

I am the arrow on its way back to the bow. The unborn are calling me from the wilderness: first a hiss, then a long, dark, mournful sound.

My guts are swollen with the fiery smoke of war and terror. And my head is full of the musty, suffocating smells of defeat, like dirty underwear boiled for a long time.

During our flight back to Kwihara I saw the eye of a vulture. That wakeful eye was looking at me from the top of a dead tree.

The war never was. It's just a sick fancy that Stanley planted in my head. The defeat is the comic reversal of his fantasies of victory.

Tomorrow we leave Kwihara and press on toward Ujiji. We'll have to make a detour around Mirambo's territory. Stanley is afraid of him.

This morning I witnessed the dressing-down Bombay gave Stanley.

"You have been deceived twice. Once by the Arabs, once by Mirambo. The third time you will die."

The blood left Stanley's face, washed through his trembling body, and returned to his reddening cheeks. His fury was about to explode through every orifice in his head, but just before the discharge it turned around and imploded instead. He looked as if he had swallowed a live rat.

When Bombay left, Stanley stood in the doorway and looked out across the plain. The white light shone around his body. He stood there for a long time and stared straight into the blinding sun without blinking.

At that moment, I felt sympathy for him. Something had changed inside him, and it made him even more alien.

Hardness and cruelty are easily acquired. Cunning and deception are more difficult, but I think he'll manage. Hardest of all is the wisdom that lets time take its course. That he will never attain.

It is noon, there is a drought in the middle of the rainy season. The weather is so hot and still that the flat plain transpires buildings, trees, entire cities that rise up steaming and disappear in the light. Rivers run around shrubs and grazing animals. Great ships bring the ocean to Unyanyembe's dry reaches. A shepherd is picked up off the ground by a frightful black giant.

The miracles of the heat do not extend to our court-yard. Here chickens stand motionless, panting for air in the narrow strip of shade next to the buildings. Some have dug themselves into the sand and fluffed themselves up so they look like carelessly made feather dusters. Right next to them lies a dog, eyes half open, sleepy with heat and the smell of chicken feathers. Goats and sheep seek cover under bushes and shrubs. Only the cows have to keep moving across the greasy frying pan of the plain.

I have lost my life but am on my way to gaining everything. Homeland, occupation, friends, pleasures, dignity, she of the soft navel, my accordion that lies dead in my room, Asmani, Saburi, Farquhar, the female figurine, Thani's cunning wisdom, and now, as we leave, Bombay's and Mama Simba's care for me. I have lost them all. The only thing I'll never lose is

Stanley, because I have never had any part of him. Stanley is everything that is not my life. Bombay is still here. I don't want to lose him, but the loss has already begun.

Tomorrow, like the houses on the plain, the ships, and the cattle, I'll lose touch with the ground and fly away from Kwihara with the streaming water.

I have stopped talking. My thoughts no longer seek an ear. When I have a sore throat, I can give a short bark or cough now and then. Sometimes I say random single words to myself: "now," "I." An involuntary sneeze is the most enjoyable. Then a cloud of happy droplets explodes from my nose and mouth.

When we left Kwihara, I was so tired that I slid off the donkey, and the ground came rushing at me and dealt my body a hard blow. Yet it didn't hurt.

The departure was noisy, as always. I heard it only from a distance, through all the ocean water that was flowing in from the hot plain. After a fall in which my head hit the ground with unusual force, my eyes focused through damp veils: right next to me I saw Bombay's curiously spindly stork's legs, higher up the black armor of his torso. A little farther away strutted Stanley the cockerel, a stream of word fragments issuing from his mouth. His metallic falsetto made the air fold in on itself and sink away in small whirlpools. Behind Stanley, the Arabs formed a landscape where turbans and fezzes were mountaintops and their garments beautifully undulating hillsides. The peaks swayed as if in prayer, and their arms waved in sup-

plicating arabesques. Stanley replied by splitting the air
into squares with his hands, packing it into cubes, and
building a wall around himself. Two Arabs came by
with a shining silver snake, a handsome slave chain to
which some of Stanley's men were attached. Their eyes
sought me out but were unable to penetrate Stanley's
wall of air. I was lifted back up onto the donkey, and
right before my eyes Stanley slipped a little knife to
Mabruki, pointing at the spot on the donkey where he
should strike. The donkey screeched and threw me off
again. Stanley's laughter fell over my face like splinters
of glass. The laughter spread to soldiers and porters.
The Arabs turned away. I thought of the time Stanley
smashed his own looking glass over my head, and then
I joined in the laughter.

Our departure was quite jolly. But I was glad that
Mama Simba wasn't there to see us.

I am the sea. I am the ship that carries the sea with it
across the continent of Africa. I rub shoulders with
mountainsides and precipices. My thoughts are clouds
above the mountain ranges. The streams flow over my
neck, the antelope prick up their ears in mine, my back
enjoys the sharp claws of the beasts of prey. I am the
sea. Trees and shrubs take root in my face, I can taste
green leaves and dry bark. Frogs croak around my
damp legs. I touch the baobab's roots with my fingertips, and my head rests in the sycamore's shade. I am
the sea. The animals gather around the acacias. My
waves have carried them there. I am the mango juice a
child licks from its black fingers. I am the water in the
cave. I am the sea.

*   *   *

Stanley is hunting. The reports of his rifle resound through the camp, and bullets whine over our heads.

When Stanley hunts, the rest of us take cover. Only the Bearer feels at home in the fusillade. He walks through it unscathed.

Once Stanley shot an antelope that was peering curiously into the muzzle of his rifle. That night he didn't sleep. He ate five kilos of meat and gave everybody an extra day of rest. I only had a little. It tasted like sweat and gunpowder and exploded right out of my rear.

Stanley wants to get at my notes. He asked me if he could see them, and I said no. He told me it was an order, and I ate the piece of paper he was pointing at. One by one, the words dropped into my stomach. It was an entertaining feeling.

Since then I amuse myself by popping a piece of paper into my mouth every time I run into him. It irritates him. He knows that I know, but he doesn't know what.

Stanley is always complaining about his ailments. I am never sick. If one part of my body gets tired, another perks up. If the day is hot, the night will be cool. When my mouth gets dry from eating, I give it water. Everything is simple and well thought out. When I am cold, I put things on; when I am warm, I take them off. When bladder and bowels are full, I empty them. When I am weary, I rest. Everything adds up. How can one be sick like Stanley? Something must be wrong with him.

For several days I have tried to write down the sound of the wilderness. It is very difficult. When I succeeded at

last, I showed Stanley the result. He didn't understand.
I even reproduced the sound of his beloved rifle when
he fired it and the sound of his bullets whizzing over
our heads. He didn't understand that either. At last I
tried the sound he most longs for: the distant thud of a
bullet entering an animal's body. He only shook his
head, and his eyes narrowed and took on a greenish
tinge.

Maybe he has gone deaf?

All that remains is hymn and spectacle, praise song and
comedy.

There are rivers here that never reach the sea. They
run out in sand and mud. If you follow them upstream,
they branch out into ever smaller rapids, brooks, rivu-
lets, but no one will find the ultimate spring, no one will
find the drop of water that is just leaving the mountain-
top to look for its kin a few millimeters farther down.

Maybe the eagle knows. It raises its spear and thrusts
at the sky.

Mornings are always happy here in Africa. The morning urine runs yellow over the dry soil. Someone shouts,
the day's first shout. A flock of weaver birds rises from a
palm tree. Nowhere is it possible to shout as beautifully
as in Africa. Shouts have to do with warm air. Warm air
that has cooled down for a moment.

What is so wild about a kudu glimpsed in a glade just
before vanishing into the underbrush? What is so wild
about a female lion drowsing in the shade of an acacia
while her cubs chase each other around?

146

When you see a hyena pull the intestine out of a living gnu, it hurts to smile. It is unfathomable. But wild? Hardly.

Stanley has decided that I should leave the expedition and return to Kwihara. His decision is firm. I don't care. I'm by myself in any case.

"Africa has been hard on you, Shaw. Your physique and character were weak to begin with. Your abused body and feeble will have not been able to resist the destructive forces of Africa. You have not been up to your task. You have not conquered a continent, it has conquered you, it has robbed you of your body and your mind."

His words were surprisingly true. Did he see so clearly, then? I was amazed by the words that came from my lips:

"Yes, I have finally lost myself."

But it wasn't me speaking. It was someone else.

On the last evening, Stanley invited me to his tent. He treated me to anything I wanted. His cook prepared roast lamb, and he himself poured me a big glass of gin. I tasted the drink: it burned my mouth and made me feel lonely and abandoned. I set the glass down, and after a while the knot of loneliness dissolved and I was able to breathe freely again. The yellow light from the lantern was pleasant, and the flickering shadows on the tent canvas were more comical than menacing.

Stanley was an anxious mother. He prattled and paced the tent. He made little gestures and funny faces to try to cheer me up. Selim ran around anxiously, dabbing at my forehead with wet napkins and wiping my mouth. When he had fussed enough, he sat down and stared at me apprehensively, as if it were in my power to destroy him.

Stanley babbled on about memories of England and laughed out loud to drive the iron rods out of his body. He threw himself on his cot, and the clay of his face cracked and fell apart in little pieces. Suddenly he sat up, became ten years old, and sang a children's song that got his face all wet. He wept and threw his arms around me and told me in a sepulchral voice that seemed to come from the privy behind the tent that the purpose of the entire expedition was to find and assist Livingstone, the old British eccentric the Arab had told us about. I burst out laughing, cheered by the thought—all this just in order to help an old man and maybe take him back to Zanzibar! It was a good thought. Whispering now, Stanley told me that the greatest difficulty lay in the fact that the old boy did not want any help and would perhaps try to flee if he heard that some white man was looking for him.

I had not understood before that Stanley had such a subtle sense of humor. This whole expedition, disguised as an exploration, was designed to find an old codger who really wanted to be left alone. I was in excellent spirits.

After a while, Stanley sent Selim to fetch my accordion. He came back quickly and put the dead instrument in my lap. It squeaked hopefully when I touched it, and Stanley begged me to play. Why not give it a try? He had actually managed to cheer me up. I played a few simple melodies, and his face slowly lengthened, and he started gulping like an animal that has taken too large a bite. In a voice that sounded as if he was about to drown, he asked me to sing a bit too. Why not? I had spoken my last words, I could now sing my last song. At his request, it was "Home, Sweet Home." In the middle of the song, he threw himself on the cot, sobbing and thrashing like a fish.

After the song I took my knife out and cut the accordion up and threw the pieces at Stanley, laughing. I thought Selim's eyes were going to roll right out of their sockets. He hastened to escort me back to my tent.

Thus ended the last jolly evening with Stanley. Outside, the night was so dark that not even loud noises could penetrate the gloom. The wilderness was totally silent.

Outside

Now I am separate from the caravan. Nevertheless, I live right inside it. I remember as through running water how Stanley ordered the soldiers to form ranks with their rifles pointed at the sky, how I was borne past on a litter and they fired a salute. It was cooler again that morning. The moisture hung heavily in the air. The soporific fragrance of rain carried me away from the camp, back to Tabora. Or did it carry me the other way, toward Ujiji?

I remember Stanley's words:

"Don't forget that you are a white man! Remember your dignity!"

Then all was silent. I heard only the porters' shuffling footsteps, their breathing, and I could smell their sweat. The morning dew dried up, the sun blazed down. Slowly I drowned in the floating honey above the savannah, in the harsh patience of the thorn bushes, the indifference of the acacias, and the dry smell of hot red soil.

I disappeared, was devoured, by a mouth that was

tight and oily. After a man's age—or was it just a few seconds?—I was born again, through an opening so wide that its edges could not be grasped. I was back in the camp. The porters who were supposed to haul me to Kwihara were now busy breaking camp and stuffing themselves with leftovers.

Everything is the same, yet so different. My eyes have become a backwards spyglass that shrinks the world to make it clearer. My arms are so short they seem useless.

I wandered about the camp to reassure myself that I really had come back. Hamadi was bidding farewell to a local beauty who sobbed inconsolably although he was showering her with gifts. Stanley was giving Selim hell for not having washed his shirts. Selim looked glum and sullen, and his omission was clearly revenge for some past injustice. The Bearer was walking circles and figure eights around his load, which looked bigger than ever. A few porters were smearing a paste on the sores on their legs while the soldiers anxiously checked their weapons. They were all mumbling to one another. I could make out the word "Mirambo" in their conversation.

I could stand in their midst without anyone so much as glancing at me. Maybe that was because I cast no shadow.

At first I couldn't see Bombay. After a while I ran into him just outside camp as he was on his way to join the others. He stopped for a few seconds and sent his killer stare straight through my skull. The whites of his eyes flashed yellow and red. A gust of wind carried with it the odor of rancid butter and rotting eggs. His lips parted, and out of the cave of his stomach rose a dry sound, like the sound of a big tree falling—first the whoosh of air and the crash of the crown on the ground, then the dull thud when the trunk performs its single drumbeat.

"Shaw."

I followed him to the tent, where he discreetly took out some food and drink. But he did not hand me the bowls of maize gruel and water, he set them on the ground a short distance from the tent, with the impersonal care of someone putting flowers on a grave.

After a couple of hours I was on my way again with the caravan. My donkey had been demoted to pack animal, and Bombay marched in my place. I was free to go anywhere I wanted. My body was without pain. I was a gas that took on the color of the surroundings: green in the forest, brownish yellow on the savannah, white in the sand dunes, red on red soil. That made me light and porous. I was gazelle and bird.

Sometimes the inverted binoculars of my eyes reversed and showed me the terrifying proximity of things. My surroundings rushed at me, and trees, grass, and people streamed through my eyes. Finally all that compacted material exploded within me. Afterward the inside of my skin was sore.

Stanley is no longer quite as solemn, even though everyone laughs at him more and more. We can't pass through a village without people running up to him pointing and laughing. He has taught himself a softer way of hating. The Wagogos have the pride of a giraffe and the arrogance of a pack of monkeys.

When I relieve myself in the mornings, I enjoy the act the way a dog enjoys his bone: slowly, patiently. I am full of dignity and humility. Under the lightening greenery of the brush or in the brownish gray morning mist of the plains, I sit on my heels and strain. My eyesight is as acute as a hawk's. The long ribbon of spent nourishment that I hold in my bowels' strong hand is slowly released. Before I deposit it on the ground in a circle, I let it return into the gut one last time.

At the edge of the forest, a herd of elephants glides by with trunks swinging in the dream. They approach us noiselessly, like clouds, and their skin is cracked dry soil. Everyone waits for the fanfare imprisoned in their bodies. When it comes it is all the more surprising.

The chameleon is the happiest of creatures. Blue at night, dark gray in the morning, then honey-gold, water and silver at noon, the ripe mango fruit in the afternoon, and finally the flame of the fire. It is only the color green it has a hard time abandoning. That is often the death of it.

How can Bombay be a Negro? What does that mean? Selim claims to be an Arab, but he is the same chatterbox of a boy who lived next door when I was a child.

What is it that joins Mama Simba, Mirambo, and the Arabs' slaves? They don't even have the same skin color. Is it the same incomprehensible thread that causes both Stanley and me to be counted as members of the human race?

On certain afternoons there is a clock in my head that strikes thunderously. How did it get to Africa? It changes color like the chameleon. Sometimes, after it has struck its green strokes, a drumming echo is heard from deep in the ground. It is the termites answering from their subterranean castles and gardens.

Stanley's expedition is a ship. The waves are howls and laughter. When they subside, only forgetfulness remains. Everything is as before. Is anyone ever going to tell their children about the rich "Arab" who was so crazy that he had no skin and had the eyes of a cat and charged ahead without even doing any business? Maybe someone will remember him for being in such a hurry that he didn't even have time for women.

I am a landscape that hates footprints. I clothe myself in thorny bushes, arm myself with snakes and scorpions. Yet there are people walking on me.

The jungle is the sanctuary of the intestines. Darkness and light entwine their fingers over the bodies of the great animals.

The monkeys remind me of Stanley. They are always exaggerating. As soon as they see us, they start screaming about the end of the world and the heavenly bodies plummeting from the sky.

Stanley runs around with his little Winchester going "bang-bang." One day he was staring after a leopard in the undergrowth. At the same time, a herd of buffalo passed behind his back. Just as he turned around, the buffalo thundered off into a clump of trees. In the meantime, the leopard showed itself and disappeared in two quick bounds. To console himself Stanley fired a few shots that were silently swallowed up by the foliage. Then everything was still for a moment, and you could hear leaves dropping to the ground. The animals listened to Stanley's heart before they set themselves in motion again.

I think he was ashamed, for the first time, that he was not an animal.

Stanley is beginning to learn the art of paying tribute. He is patient and mostly lets Bombay do the negotiating. In his light blue eyes, which are rarely moistened by their lids, strident stupidity has assumed a melancholy overlay of experience. But the brutal curve of his mouth and mustache still has a lot to learn. It came close to starting a war with a greedy chieftain. But a yellowish streak of cunning in the old man's eyes made Stanley listen to Bombay and continue negotiations.

Today I heard the roar of Lake Tanganyika. Bombay told Stanley that when there is a strong wind, great caves on the far side of the lake produce a bellowing that sometimes resembles distant thunder. Stanley stared in the direction of the sound, and his face hardened even as tears streamed from his eyes. He pointed a finger, opened his mouth to say something, but his lips were completely mute.

Now Stanley has full control over the caravan of forty men. Even Bombay is just a tool in his hands. There are moments when I regret that I stand outside his blind faith, his confidence, his yearning for something more, his certainty that there is a goal and that this wandering is a duty.

I too would like to make myself at home in an imagined future. But I am the arrow on its way back to the bow.

Stanley has swallowed his image of himself. Success will be the cross he has to bear. The taste of iron will remain forever on his tongue. The armor is beginning to shine. He still says "Father Livingstone" with a catch in his voice, but the melancholy look he had after the war has disappeared.

He is a man, and he is preparing himself for his wedding.

This morning Stanley surpassed himself. Without a shred of hesitation he made a decision that saved the entire caravan. For the first time his resolution joined hands with his strange whims, and for the first time I saw the possibilities in the man.

A couple of hours before sunrise the caravan started out on a forced march through the final miles of hostile Uhha territory. Everybody was in good spirits. Hunger, disease, war, and death were behind now. Ahead, only a few days' march away, lay the goal: Ujiji.

No one spoke in the cool of the morning. They walked quickly and with determination. The goats had been muzzled so that their bleating wouldn't betray the caravan. At sunrise the muzzles were cut, and everyone began talking loudly and happily. At that very moment Stanley and the guide, Hamadi, strode right into a village that was just waking up to a new day. Stanley ordered a halt and asked Hamadi for advice. The latter only shook his head with a panic-stricken look. Stanley spun on his heel and gave orders that spread through the caravan with amazing speed. In less than fifteen seconds, everybody knew that the animals had to be slaughtered, and within a minute all the caravan's goats and chickens had breathed their last.

A few villagers watched as if in a dream, paralyzed. Only after the strangers had disappeared again did they wake up their neighbors. No one thought of pursuing the caravan. They approached the animal carcasses hesitantly, as if fearing an ambush. Thunderstruck, they stood and stared at these scattered gifts, unable to decide whether they were a good omen or a bad.

The caravan passed silently and swiftly through the jungle along the wide elephant paths. After an hour's march the forest ended, and an undulating plain spread out before them. The sun climbed higher in the sky and scattered the fog in the valley. It rose like smoke before dissipating against the surrounding mountainsides.

The caravan came to a halt. The loads were softly lowered to the ground. Someone sang a couple of notes, and then all joined in a many-voiced African hymn, in its rugged sadness shot through with joy the most beautiful sound the human ear can hear. Stanley stood at the head of the caravan and looked out over the gentle landscape with stiff neck and a tensed jaw. His body's posture was an elaborately lettered script: for once to have been one with your men, for once to have been a genius, for once to have taken the step from the hope, naiveté, and sentimentality of youth to the hardness and imposing isolation of manhood. Between clay and jar, between fire and iron.

He turned when the song was over and waved his order to depart. When the porters and soldiers were ready, he curtly announced that they would all receive a bonus of a doti of cloth upon arrival in Ujiji. He turned his back on the men's cheers and strode quickly down into the valley, on his way to Lake Tanganyika and its holy man.

One porter has a small wound on his leg, hardly more than a scratch. A drop of blood oozes out. The man wipes it off with his hand, without looking at the wound. He goes on talking to his comrade.

I am the only one who sees that the scratch will be the death of him, I am the only one who can't do anything about it.

Stanley is in an excellent mood. He is busy taking measurements of the porters' skulls and the length of their legs. All is meticulously recorded. Some of the porters grin with embarrassment, others seem to believe that the examination will protect them and bow their heads worshipfully.

When Stanley measured Bombay's head, he couldn't believe the figures and repeated the procedure several times.

I am the sea again.

I watch a woman bend down and lift a jar up onto her head. She is on her way to the river. The water lies waiting, smooth and prayerful.

The woman bends down so that her breasts sway. With one hand on her child's arm she lifts it up and settles it on her hip. The child pinches the shiny black upper arms and inhales the mother's sour fragrance.

The woman stops, stretches her arms to the sky, loosens her shawl, and knots it again. Her back arches, her breasts harden, the thicket of her armpits glistens, and her arms form a lute with her head as the sound box.

The woman does not stay, nor the jar, nor the child, nor the shawl. Nothing stays.

One must not kill people or animals or trees. One must only point at the air with an imaginary spear. Not even the children understand this.

The night has many faces. Weep, Mother. The Gods carry tomorrow on their backs. Weep for your children who have been flogged and beaten and taken away by strangers. Weep on your field, on your firewood, over your newborn child. Somewhere the Gods are singing so that the giraffes will fall asleep, the rhinoceroses will mate, the grass will grow green in the dry season.

Kill or be killed. They shall remember your naked footprints on the path, your laughter by the fire, and the cool water in your cupped hand.

Today I milked a few drops of semen into a blood puddle where the soldiers had slaughtered a goat. White and red. Beautiful and innocent.

* * *

The most important thing I have lost has no name. It is around me constantly. Around the tree trunks, deep in the underbrush, hidden in the grass. It is a hollow well with the voice of a child or an old man.

Sometimes I catch a glimpse of it on the far side of a hut, a bush, a group of men. I rush over, but I always get there too late.

My favorite pastime is listening to the porters' and soldiers' stories around the fire at night. I don't know the language, but I understand anyway. I am amused when it is time to laugh, I shake my head when trouble threatens, I wave my hands wildly in the face of exaggeration. It is remarkable how much they can embroider those stories.

Stanley is so restless that he eats standing up, sleeps standing up, and even walks "standing up," perfectly erect, as if he intended to move vertically instead of horizontally. His agitation spreads through the caravan like ants. At the evening fire, the men find it difficult to settle down. They are constantly throwing wood on the flames, which burn out of control and keep everyone busy damping them down again. No one cooks anymore. Meat and vegetables are eaten raw, and people defecate wherever they happen to be. Everyone talks like Stanley, in short, peremptory phrases. This morning they started imitating Stanley's movements and gestures too. They went around giving each other orders, strutting about as if they had boots on their feet and riding crops in their hands. Into the midst of this stilted dance strode Stanley himself, like a cock in a henhouse, to demonstrate the correct way of performing the movements. After a while he shouted that he and he alone was Stanley. They all shouted back that they and they alone were Stanley. In the end it was decided that the one who had a real donkey whip in his tent had the right to call himself Stanley.

A cloud of morning dew floats around my head. I walk into the forest to find the woman who disappeared. She is naked and black and eats juicy fruits. I will suckle her with my member.

Stanley climbs a hill to get a better view of Lake Tanganyika. He wants to be alone. At the top he goes down on bended knee, stretches his arms to the sky, and speaks with a flapping motion. He is trying to fly. The porters laugh so hard that their spittle soaks me. They imitate him and howl with laughter. When Stanley comes back down, they run off to enjoy their merriment a little longer. At the campsite he paces, solitary, and stares about in bewilderment. When the laughter starts up again and washes over him from the surrounding bushes, fear flares up in his eyes. But he recovers quickly when Bombay comes lumbering back like a rhinoceros with a bad conscience.

My skull is an eggshell lit from within. This thin shell is the border between *then* and *thereafter*. Every second, *then* threatens to carve its way out with a razor's edge and become *thereafter*. Every second, *thereafter* threatens to push through the shell and merge with *then*. That is why I carry my head high, with care.

Now is the wind. I am the wind. Everything else is also the wind. Everything is us. Everywhere.

Stanley is trying to teach the soldiers to stand to attention. It isn't going well. When they draw themselves up and stand motionless, laughter starts like a cramp in their feet, spirals up through the skinny legs, takes a few turns through their guts, and finally explodes out of their mouths.

Stanley surprises them while they are eating, pissing, sleeping, fighting, picking splinters out of their feet. Atten-tion! After only a day their laughter vanished and their bodies stiffened as if they had just been hit by a rifle bullet.

Bombay thumbs his nose at all this rigmarole. Nevertheless, he is no longer the same man. Something was left behind with Mama Simba.

Now we are there. At our destination.

The caravan raced down into Ujiji like a class without a teacher. Stanley went solemnly, but even he occasionally skipped like a schoolgirl and shouted *yambo* at the startled villagers.

Lake Tanganyika is the womb of Africa. It smells of sex, fish, and fresh water.

A dignified group of Arabs stood waiting for us in the town square. They welcomed us and invited Stanley into a magnificent building, but he shook his head and asked for the white man Livingstone. The Arabs conferred discreetly and shouted something to a couple of boys, who ran off to a small hut. Before they reached it, a strange figure staggered forth and set out on a limping run to the water's edge. The boys cut him off, and he turned and hopped back through the dark doorway of the hut. He looked like an injured bird that couldn't fly. When the Arab boys went into the hut after him, a few shrill shouts were heard. Then all was silence. After a minute or two—Stanley stood stamping in the dust, chewing his froth-flecked lips—all three emerged from the hut. The boys were holding the man by the arms. He resembled a chimpanzee. His legs were skinny and bowed, his arms thin as if someone had stretched them. Hair and beard were gray and matted, the black mouth opened and closed without a sound. A string of spittle shone at the corner of it, and the moist eyes were wide open, as if after a lingering horror. He was dressed in dirty rags and hobbled along on bare feet that were knobby and sore from dust-flea bites.

When they led the old fellow up to Stanley, Stanley's chin was shaking as if it were about to take leave of his skull. One of the Arab boys took the old man's right arm and presented a clawlike hand, which Stanley clasped between his own. He went down on his knees, kissed the claw, and wept, pressing it to his cheek. The Arabs turned away, embarrassed.

Then Stanley got to his feet again slowly.

"Dr. Livingstone, I presume."

The old wretch barked a little laugh but then looked terrified again. Stanley wound one of the stiff apelike arms around his shoulders and led Livingstone back to the hut. In the shadow of the protruding palm-leaf roof they sank down onto a straw mat covered with a couple of goatskins.

Always prepared, Selim appeared with a small table

163

on which he placed two silver goblets and a bottle of Sillery champagne. Stanley popped the cork, and the old man gave a spastic jerk. The wine was poured. Livingstone's animal eyes watched everything from a great distance, as if witnessing an old memory. Stanley raised the silver goblet to Livingstone's mouth, and he tasted the light, bubbly liquid fearfully, smacking his lips a couple of times before his face crinkled into an obscene grin. Then, with surprising agility, he reached for the goblet and drained it in a couple of loud gulps. Stanley watched it all as if he were witnessing a miracle.

A short while later, Livingstone fell asleep on one of the goatskins. His head was resting on Stanley's knee. The Arabs bowed respectfully and walked away, bemused and conversing in low voices. Stanley waved to Bombay and ordered him to unpack and see to it that everybody had food, drink, and lodging for the night. The porters and soldiers retired to their tasks, whispering among themselves. Only a few children stayed and stared mutely at the two white men.

Stanley sat there for a couple of hours. Then the old man woke up and retreated to the darkness of the hut without saying a word.

Livingstone and I have been sitting and staring into each other's faces. His is vacant, reflecting only the dead calm inside him. Finally he threw a little sand at me.

Stanley gives a lecture that lasts for days. Grant has been elected president, the Suez Canal has been opened, the Trans-Pacific Railroad has been completed, the rebellion on Crete has been crushed, Prussia has annexed Schleswig-Holstein and threatened Denmark, and Bismarck has routed Napoleon. Isabella has been ousted from the throne of Spain, and freedom of religion has been debated among the disciples of the so-called Enlightenment.

Stanley speaks long and well. He is as knowledgeable as a book and as eloquent as a member of Parliament. Livingstone sits next to him picking at scraps of food and scratching his legs. He laughs when Stanley laughs and shakes his head when Stanley expresses concern about the convulsions of the world.

This morning Livingstone spoke his first words.

"What art thou doing here?" he asked.

His voice was metallic and sounded as if it came from somewhere just behind him.

"I came here to find you, Dr. Livingstone, and to offer you any assistance you may need."

Livingstone peeked about as if searching for something; he looked like he had been caught doing something shameful. A slightly pained expression came over his face. He rose to his feet, hobbled down to the lake, and sat there gazing out over it.

Stanley does calisthenics every morning before going to Livingstone's hut to act as his servant. Every morning he brings some object from his own house. His voice rattles on incessantly from dawn to dusk.

Now and again Livingstone leaves his hut to go sit by the lake. Sometimes the Arabs and other natives sit next to him and talk to him in low voices. The enormous, resonant body of water bounces their words off the walls of Ujiji. Then Stanley comes running, rigid with anxiety, worry, and jealousy.

In a corner of Livingstone's hut Stanley has found a powerful O'Reilly rifle. Every day he asks Livingstone for permission to borrow it. Then he sits under a tree, cleaning the weapon and playing with it.

One morning Livingstone came out of his hut cradling something in his arms. He carried it to the back of the house like a monkey that has found a treasure and wants to examine it undisturbed. Stanley stood to one side and cried like a child. The object Livingstone was carrying was a Bible. Stanley stopped crying when Livingstone started eating the pages.

I am trying to win Livingstone's heart by sitting near him and remaining completely quiet. Judging from his expression, he feels comfortable with that. I blow on his sores, lend him my shoulder when he wants to get up, assist him when he is eating. His stomach is filled with tar and stones. At the latrine I support him as he crouches there panting and straining with every sinew in his spidery body. His intestines are a marble snake, his arsehole is a raisin. When he is done, I help him unfold his creaking joints and legs so that he can make his own way back to the hut.

The smell of fresh water is so strong at times that it is intoxicating. I reel around between the huts of Ujiji, drunk and happy.

*   *   *

Livingstone gives his food away. The village children flock to his hut when he is eating, and he lets them help themselves. The scene reminds me of an apathetic old beast of prey letting the vultures partake of the kill. At first Stanley stood watching with amusement, but on the second day he threw stones at the children to chase them off. He also admonished Livingstone to show more concern for his own welfare.

Stanley has moved into Livingstone's hut. They sleep in the same bed, and Stanley plays house. During meals he can be both child and father. Poor Selim has found refuge with an ugly old Arab. Livingstone has spoken to me at last. We were sitting down by the lake, and the freshwater smell was slightly stale, warm and humid. The calm water surface curved away in an arc. A short distance from us some fishermen were pulling their canoes ashore. Across the lake we could see hazy mountains, or were they clouds? Right behind us some pigs were rooting in the ground, grunting.

He had been clearing his throat all day, and I understood that something was on its way. The minutes grew longer and longer, and when the sun began to dim on the far side of the lake I got worried that no words would be spoken that day after all.

When they finally came, they were heavy as stones and went hopping out of his black mouth like frogs. His body became more and more shriveled as he spoke, his skin collapsing into the vacuum the words had left.

"We shall go on an exploratory expedition on Lake Tanganyika, Stanley and I. We are playing. I must play again. I used to play that the Lualaba ran north. If it runs west, someone else must play that. Such is my life.

The Negroes have been hospitable to me. As have the slave traders, even though they have destroyed every Negro family I ever met. Because they care for me, the Negroes have spoken the name of Jesus and sung songs about him. But since they live in the jungle, their god lives in the jungle too. Those who live on the plains say that he lives on the plains. I have seen him there myself. In Africa the mothers carry their children next to their naked bodies, and they miss them like an amputated arm when they are stolen and sold. Once a lion bit my shoulder. It did not hurt." Here he laughed. "My native tongue trickled away with the rivers. Stanley brought it here again, but I no longer speak it. It sounds frightful. That is why I cannot return to my homeland. Here I have no need to speak. I can live among the Arabs, Negroes, pigs, and chickens. They are good to me. The children irritate me sometimes. Stanley has a habit of waking me up at night. He sleeps fitfully, he is afraid of being alone, he is afraid of silence. He is a big-child, and they will call him a great man. I knew that he would find me. He needs me. To him I am the soft fingertips of his firm hand, the gentle smile on his determined face. Once I bore within me a raging passion that was so great only the African continent could contain it. But Africa devoured it. It was not enough. Yet the passion brought with it a monster that has only begun to show its face. I am afraid of that monster. Here in Ujiji I have felt safe. Now I do not know. I may well have to start moving again. After all, I am Livingstone." Another laugh. "All that remains of me is an ear. I am an ear. I used to be a mouth as large as a cathedral. My will to help and serve was so great that I almost disap-

peared on the banks of the winding rivers. I straightened the watercourses, gave them shortcuts, opened up
valleys for them. The crocodiles yawned, the hippopotamuses submerged with a snort, and the brown
water always flowed the wrong way. I drew maps up and
down, let north become south, traveled backwards or
sideways like a crab. I asked a question of every tree,
and their names were as numerous as their leaves. Villages had different names depending on the direction
from which one approached them, rivers changed
names along stretches no one was able to show me,
there was a river ghost for every canoe, and everyone
laughed at my questions. I told them about a desert god
from the Near East and about his kindly son. I gave
words to a love that is wordless. Into the Negroes' inex-
haustible storehouse of gods and spirits my god disappeared, accepted and tolerated to the point of
anonymity and muteness among all the others. They
listened to me and offered me food and wives. They
asked my god for help against the slave traders, believ-
ing that there was a geographical connection between
them. And I too was swallowed up by these people and
this landscape. I dried out in the heat and swelled in
the tremendous rains. I am an ear. I have no brain left,
scarcely any sensation, only hearing, and even that is
beginning to desert me. My mouth is parched, my
passion wanders about alone like a restless jungle ghost,
and I am content to hold a few crumbs of earth in my
hand. And now we shall go out and explore again. Our
eyes will create waterways, mountains, tribes, villages. I
know what is expected of me. I do not wish it, but I am
Livingstone, and I must carry that yoke until the day I

die. But I will not leave the interior. I dare not. The terror I feel when Stanley talks about Europe gives me stomach cramps. I do not know my family, and I never think about them anymore. But I am lonely. As lonely as a man can be. And tired."

With that he stopped. While he was still speaking, I heard Stanley call his name. Not far from us a few soldiers were looking for him on the shore. We sat in the shade of a bush, and no one found us. It grew dark while he was speaking, and when he had finished, it was night. He had hardly uttered the last word, "tired," when he curled up and fell asleep in the sand. His snoring was strangely dark and sonorous to come from a body as desiccated as his was.

I sat next to him for a couple of hours. Then I went and woke Bombay. Without looking at me or saying a word he followed me to the beach, picked up the light body, and carried it back to the hut. There sat Stanley, beside himself with anxiety. Bombay put his snoring burden into Stanley's arms, and he carefully laid it on their shared bed. Then Stanley fetched his Winchester rifle and gave it to Bombay without a word.

A few days later they left Ujiji by boat to travel to the northern reaches of the lake. Livingstone was decked out as an explorer, with khaki suit, topee, and a rifle. He looked like a circus animal dressed up as a person, and his newly shaven cheeks were as naked as a plucked chicken.

The British and American flags fluttered languidly in the sterns of the two boats. The oarsmen were driven to their places with the donkey whip, and the provisions were stowed. The soldiers fired a salute, the Arabs raised their hands in farewell. A little farther away stood the Negroes in massed ranks, and among them I caught a glimpse of Bombay. His sullen eyes were easy to distinguish among all the curious gazes. Some soldiers managed to find him too, and they forced him down to Stanley's boat. He was shouldering the Winchester—a useless weapon, as everyone knew, since Stanley had not given him any ammunition for it. After a lash from Stanley's whip he took his place in the boat.

There was something striking about Livingstone. It was very pronounced. His face shone with contentment. His movements were measured and highly dignified. He even pointed out to Stanley a box of provisions that was almost left behind on the beach.

Slowly the boats set out, and the oarsmen began their work. Stanley and Livingstone stood in the sterns of their respective boats, one under the American flag, the other under the British flag. They did not sit down until they could no longer be seen from Ujiji.

The warm hand and the cold, the soft and the hard. The son has found his father, and the father has become his son's son, the son his father's father. They will be invincible.

When the boats disappeared, I disappeared too. I am no longer. I have nothing to do with events. I am only writing this. For the last time I fly low over Lake Tanganyika, and the scent of sex and fresh water streams through me. It is dusk. In the middle of the lake the backs of the whales rise out of the lukewarm water, and almost inaudible cries go out like needles to all points of the compass. After a few seconds' glassy silence the answer comes, from north and south, east and west, from the South Atlantic, the Indian Ocean, and the Mediterranean: cries from cold green salt water, exact descriptions of travel, singing diagrams of temperature, winds, humidity, and ocean currents. Like a thought, the whales dive toward the bottom of the lake, toward the lower firmament, away from memory without shores and warmth, and down to the cool gorge where the water rises in a tree of bubbles.

At night the savannah takes long deep breaths. The hyenas pick up their pace. At the waterholes frogs croak. A herd of impala starts and listens. A herd of elephants shuffles into a swamp.

The woman sits up in bed. She leaves the man and the damp, tangled sheets and goes alone into the night.

Perhaps there never were any whales in Lake Tanganyika. What do I care.

Now the hissing steals across the surface of the water on dry feet. From the far side of the lake come the slowly dying lamentations of the caves. I recognize the sound only too well.

Then the great clock of silence. The sea.

The sea has always frightened me.